F
J
    Kenny, Campbell
       Trixie Belden, the
Mystery of the Queen's
Necklace

    FILED ON SHELF UNDER
    CAMPBELL, JULIE

TRIXIE BELDEN.

The TRIXIE BELDEN Series

TRIXIE BELDEN®

THE MYSTERY OF THE QUEEN'S NECKLACE

By Kathryn Kenny

A GOLDEN BOOK • NEW YORK

Western Publishing Company, Inc., Racine, Wisconsin 53404

CONTENTS

THE MYSTERY OF THE QUEEN'S NECKLACE

Honey's Inheritance • 1

TRIXIE BELDEN'S blue eyes were stormy. She and her family were assembled around the kitchen table at Crabapple Farm, having what Trixie called a council of war. Her parents and her older brothers, Brian and Mart, were present—everyone except six-year-old Bobby.

"I want to play war, too," he had insisted.

"Not as long as you're the interrupting-est little boy in Westchester County, New York!" Trixie had told him, too upset to be more tactful. "Why don't you go outside and play with Reddy? He could certainly use the exercise."

Fortunately, that suggestion had appealed to him,

which meant that Trixie was free, she hoped, to present her arguments in relative peace and quiet.

"Now, what's this all about?" her father wanted to know, looking up from the newspaper.

Trixie took a deep breath and gathered her thoughts. A trip to England—that was what it was all about! The parents of Trixie's best friend, Honey Wheeler, had offered to take the Bob-Whites of the Glen with them on their trip to England the following week. Besides Trixie and Honey, the Bob-Whites included Brian, Mart, Diana Lynch, Dan Mangan, and Honey's adoptive brother, Jim Frayne. The semi-secret club had shared many good times together all over the United States, but never before had they been across the ocean. So far, however, Trixie's parents had maintained that such an expensive trip was out of the question for the Belden young people. But Trixie Belden was not one to give up an argument that easily.

"Well," she said finally, "I just don't think it's fair for you and Moms to say that Brian and Mart and I can't go to England, till you hear all the reasons." *Like the fact that Honey will be crushed if I'm not allowed to go*, Trixie thought to herself. *And the fact that Jim is going, and it'll be so much fun. . . .*

"Let's hear your reasons," Peter Belden said in his most businesslike voice.

"For one thing," Trixie began, and then she noticed that her father was sneaking a look at the

14

newspaper! "Mo-oms," Trixie protested, and Helen Belden reached over and gently removed his reading glasses.

"I'm listening," he said with a grin. "But, as I told you before, there's no way you kids can afford a trip abroad, and the Wheelers have done too much for this family already."

"But, Dad," Trixie pleaded, "Mr. and Mrs. Wheeler have tons of money, and they're going on business anyway and taking their own private plane, like when they took us to St. Louis and when they sent us to Vermont, so it wouldn't cost all that much, and besides, Honey says her parents are always saying that they'll never be able to do enough for the Beldens, because when Honey first moved here, she was so lonesome and sickly and scared of practically everything, and now she's so healthy and has so many friends, and—"

"Whoa!" chuckled Mr. Belden. "How many reasons was that?"

" 'I would my horse had the speed of your tongue,' " Mart quoted dryly. He had recently written a paper for his English class on *Much Ado About Nothing*, and ever since then he'd considered himself the ultimate expert on Shakespeare, especially on quotations of his work.

"My tongue happens to be speaking for you, too, you know," Trixie told her brother indignantly.

Always ready for an argument, Trixie and Mart

were almost the same age. At fifteen, he was eleven months older. They looked very much alike, too, with their mother's sandy blond hair and bright blue eyes, and their own personal freckles. People who didn't know them often thought they were twins. Lately, with Mart letting his short hair grow out, the resemblance was even closer, much to Mart's dismay. Deep down he was one of Trixie's staunchest supporters, but he did enjoy needling her. One of the ways Trixie got back at him was to tease him about being her almost-twin.

"You don't have to speak for me, Trix," said Brian as he selected an apple from a big bowl of fruit on the red-checked tablecloth. "I already told you, I've got to stay home and work." Brian was seventeen, with dark hair and eyes like his father's, and he was more serious than the "almost-twins." He was planning to be a doctor, and he needed every cent he could earn for medical school.

"I almost forgot," sighed Trixie. "But just because you have to work, and Dan has to work, and Di has to go to Milwaukee with her parents doesn't mean that I shouldn't get to see the world until—until I'm old and stodgy!"

"Brian has a point, though," said Mrs. Belden. "You all do have responsibilities here at home."

"I know, Moms," Trixie said quickly. "But Mrs. Wheeler really *wants* us to be with Honey and Jim while she and Mr. Wheeler tend to their business.

Sure, they've taken us on trips before, but we took Honey and Jim to Uncle Andrew's lodge in the Ozarks and the sheep farm in Iowa, and it was Di Lynch's family that took us all to Washington, D.C., and Williamsburg and Arizona. And you know how the Bob-Whites always help a lot of people on our trips—"

"Not to mention, Schoolgirl Shamus," Mart interrupted her breathless recital, "how you always manage to fathom all those unfathomable mysteries."

"It isn't just me," Trixie said. "It's me and Honey and all the Bob-Whites." She didn't add that she and Honey were going to establish their own detective agency when they got out of school, because everybody knew that.

Mrs. Belden shook her head regretfully as she got up to take a batch of brownies out of the oven. Mr. Belden reached for the newspaper.

"Wait!" Trixie protested. "I'm not finished yet!" Her war council was turning into a total fiasco. Apparently, her parents had never had any intention of changing their minds.

Trixie looked ready to explode, and Brian nudged her under the table.

"Douse the dynamite," he said softly. "It won't do any good to blow up."

"I'm afraid the subject is closed," Mr. Belden said, and Trixie could almost hear the definite click of a vault door swinging shut in the First National Bank

17

of Sleepyside, where her father worked.

"I'm sure you'll get to England sometime," Mrs. Belden said, her blue eyes warm with sympathy. "But in the meantime, how about some brownies?"

One whiff of the fudgy brownies was enough to make Mart forget everything else, and Brian was already cutting his first serving. But Trixie felt that what she needed at the moment was cool air, not hot brownies.

"I'm going over to Honey's for a while," she mumbled. "Okay?"

"I'll be over in a few minutes," promised Mart in between bites.

"All right," their mother said. "But be home early."

Trixie fairly flew up the footpath that led from Crabapple Farm to the Manor House, high on the hill. Every minute that she and Honey had left was precious. She had so many questions. When were they leaving? How long were they going to stay? Not all summer, she hoped. That would be awful!

As Trixie neared the top of the hill, Honey came flying down to meet her. Her honey-blond hair streamed out behind her, and her hazel eyes were enormous.

"Trixie!" she cried. "Just wait till you see what I've got!"

"Why do I have to see it?" demanded Trixie breathlessly. "Just tell me!"

"You'd never believe me, that's why," said Honey,

leading the way up to the white mansion on the Hudson River hilltop.

"I'll die if you don't tell me right this minute," Trixie threatened as they hurried up the steps of the veranda that encircled the house.

"Oh, Trixie, you're always dying," Honey laughed. "I'll give you some clues, though. It's all different colors, and it's very, *very* old."

The girls rushed inside and almost bumped into Mrs. Wheeler, who was in the reception hall talking to one of the maids. *Uh-oh*, Trixie thought to herself. *Slow down.* Honey's mother was very nice, but Trixie couldn't help feeling a little in awe of her. She never had a hair out of place, it seemed, and she was always dressed up, even for riding. She came from a socially prominent family, and she always looked as perfect as she did in the oil portrait of her in the Wheeler living room.

Trixie felt different toward Honey's redheaded father. He was a millionaire in his own right and had built up a far-flung business empire, but somehow all the Bob-Whites felt as comfortable with him as they did with their own fathers. *Or maybe more so*, Trixie thought grumpily. She wasn't too comfortable with her own father at the moment.

"Good evening, Trixie," Mrs. Wheeler said. "I suppose you have come to see Honey's—"

"Don't tell," Honey said. "I want to surprise her."

"Very well, dear." Mrs. Wheeler smiled at them.

"Why don't you take her up to your room? The—that is, it—has come back from the jeweler's, and I left it in your top dresser drawer. They did a beautiful job of cleaning and polish—"

"Mo-therrr," Honey warned, pulling Trixie after her up the broad, crimson-carpeted stairway. The carpet was new—Mrs. Wheeler loved to redecorate— but the gleaming cherry wood banisters would never change. The Manor House was modeled after the Dutch settlements that had been built on the Hudson before the American Revolution. It was certainly magnificent, but Trixie never dreamed of trading it for her own small farmhouse in the hollow below. Everybody loved Crabapple Farm.

Honey's room was done in white, with a ruffled organdy bedspread and curtains to match. Trixie had been a little in awe of it, too, at first, but no more.

"Now," Trixie demanded, plopping down on the bed, "if you don't show me whatever-it-is right this minute, I'll—I'll—" Not being able to think of anything worse than her usual death scene, she subsided. Besides, Honey was already opening her bureau drawer and taking out a moth-eaten purple velvet box.

"It's something I just inherited," said Honey. "From my great-great-aunt Priscilla, whom I never even knew. Mother just faintly remembers her, from when she was a little girl and went to visit her in New England. My great-great-aunt was terribly old even

20

then. She's been in a rest home, and she just died last spring—at the age of ninety-nine.''

"Gleeps," Trixie said. "That's ancient. It's too bad she didn't make it to a hundred so she could be a centennial."

"I think you mean a centenarian," Honey said. "You and your near-miss vocabulary."

"Whatever," Trixie said hastily. "Just tell me— *what* did you inherit?"

"This!" Honey snapped open the old box with a flourish and spilled its contents out onto the bed. Huge sapphires, emeralds, and rubies sparkled against the snow-white bedspread. They were set in a thick gold chain encrusted with diamonds and pearls.

"Yipes!" Trixie whispered. "Are they real?"

"Mother had them appraised," Honey said. "She didn't think they were, but she wasn't sure, because they were all gucked up before she had them cleaned. She said if they *were* real, they ought to be locked up in the Tower of London with the crown jewels. Nobody but kings and queens would wear something like this."

"Fortunately," Mrs. Wheeler said from the open doorway, "they turned out to be only imitations."

"Fortunately?" Trixie gasped. "You mean they're fake? And you're *glad* of it?"

Honey slipped the heavy, glittering necklace over her head. It hung in a wide circle almost to her waist. "Doesn't look much like junk jewelry, does it?" she said. She struck a pose for Trixie's benefit.

Mrs. Wheeler sat down in a white-ruffled rocker. "The stones are not real, but the piece still may be valuable, particularly if it turns out to have any special historical interest. The appraiser assures us that it is very old."

"As old as your aunt Priscilla?" Trixie asked.

"Older than that," Mrs. Wheeler said.

"It might go back to the days of Queen Elizabeth," Honey said. "Queen Elizabeth the First, that is. That's over four *hundred* years."

Trixie gulped.

"That remains to be seen," Mrs. Wheeler said, smiling at their excitement.

"That's what I was just coming down to Crabapple Farm to tell you." Honey's eyes glowed. "Now you just *have* to come to England with us, Trix—you and Mart, even if Brian can't come. Because we have to trace the necklace, and we already know that it comes from England! Miss Trask will come with us— she used to teach history as well as math before she came to be my governess—and there are a lot of old libraries where we can look up stuff, like my mother's ancestors, and the jewelry of different periods, and all. Besides, my dad says that if we're going to solve a mystery, there's nobody who can do that better than Trixie Belden."

"Our supersleuth!" came a cheerful voice from Honey's open door.

It was Jim, and right behind him, in the hall, was Mart. Trixie was about to burst already, from all sorts of mixed-up emotions, and the sight of Jim's friendly face and tousled red hair was almost too much.

"But we can't go with you," she wailed. "My parents say it's absolutely out of the qu-question." She blinked back tears, determined not to cry in front of Jim, who was always saying how spunky she was.

"Perhaps Matthew and I could pay a little call on your parents," Mrs. Wheeler suggested. "We could explain how much we need the, er, the Belden-Wheeler Detective Agency, to trace the origin of the necklace." Trixie could have sworn she saw a twinkle in Mrs. Wheeler's eyes. "And it would mean a great deal to me to find out more about my ancestors, too."

"You mean like a *job?* For the agency?" Honey cried. "Oh, Trixie, wouldn't that be fabulous? A real assignment!"

"Your others have certainly been *un*real," Mart commented.

Trixie was speechless. The Belden-Wheeler Detective Agency was so far just a dream, for when she and Honey grew up. Of course, they had solved quite a few mysteries already, with the help of all the Bob-Whites, but those had been mostly accidental. . . .

"I suppose this would be an all-expenses-paid assignment?" Jim drawled, still leaning against the doorjamb.

23

"Expenses!" Trixie gasped. "Oh, my sainted aunt!"

"That's *my* sainted aunt," Honey put in.

"All expenses would be paid," Mrs. Wheeler assured them. "Keep a record of them."

"Pinch me," Trixie said dreamily. "Nope—on second thought, don't pinch me. I might wake up."

"What's the name of the family you want us to trace?" Mart asked, curious. "Is it Wheeler?"

"No, it's my family," Mrs. Wheeler said. "My maiden name is Hart. *H-a-r-t.* I believe there's a connection with the Shakespeares, way back."

"You're kidding!" exclaimed Mart.

"You like Shakespeare?" Mrs. Wheeler asked. "I'm glad. I expect you'll be staying in Stratford-on-Avon, his birthplace, for at least a few days. We'll arrange for you to see one or two of his plays at the Royal Shakespeare Theatre." She stood up. "I'm going to go hunt up Matthew right now."

Mrs. Wheeler hurried out of the room, and Trixie let out a sigh. "Oh, Honey, your mom is absolutely super," she said. "Do you really think they can talk my parents into it?"

"I have a hunch they can," Mart said confidently. "And I can see it all now in *The Sleepyside Sun:* 'The Belden-Wheeler Detective Agency took off on a private jet today for the British Isles, where they will function as genealogical shamuses in an attempt to discover the origin of a splendiferous bauble. Also under investigation will be the extraction of Miss

Madeleine Wheeler's materfamilial roots.' "

"Oh, Mart, you make it sound like we're going to the dentist," said Honey, giggling.

Trixie shivered with excitement. To England! Would she really get to go? *Well, even if I don't,* she thought stubbornly, *the Belden-Wheeler Detective Agency is still going to solve the mystery of Honey's inheritance . . . somehow.*

Yankee, Go Home · 2

IT WAS THE BOB-WHITES' first day in London, and already they were hopelessly lost.

After getting the young people settled in a small bed-and-breakfast hotel on the previous night, Mr. and Mrs. Wheeler had gone on to Paris. Trixie felt she'd be eternally grateful to them for talking her parents into allowing her and Mart to accompany Honey and Jim. Once they were convinced that Trixie and Mart would be a genuine help on the trip, Mr. and Mrs. Belden had revised their verdict and decided that it would be wonderfully educational. Trixie still had to pinch herself from time to time to make sure she really was on the opposite side of the Atlantic, and not just in some unusually pleasant dream!

Miss Trask was spending the first day doing preliminary research on the Hart family at the English Birth Registry, which meant that the Bob-Whites were beginning their sight-seeing adventures on their own.

By the middle of the morning, they had covered a lot of territory—mostly underground territory. The tube, as the Londoners called their honeycomb of subways, was jammed with English commuters and foreign sightseers. Trains roared in all directions through the dimly lighted tunnels, and it seemed that nobody could tell the Americans which train they should take.

"Everything is so much fun in London, even being lost," said Trixie. "But, gleeps, I don't think the English people like us very much."

"What makes you say that?" Honey demanded.

"Didn't you hear what that man called us?" Trixie asked. "The one who pushed us onto this train when we didn't know if it was the right one or not?"

"Bloody tourists," recalled Mart.

"I'm sure that doesn't mean that they don't like us," Honey said. "They're probably just in a hurry to get to their jobs."

"Honey, you'd defend a snake if it bit you," chuckled Jim. Before Honey could protest, he went on, "Well, I don't care where we are. I think we should get off at the next station. I'm getting homesick for daylight. I'm not used to traveling underground."

The next station, according to the sign on the gleaming white tile wall, turned out to be Baker Street. The other Bob-Whites gladly agreed to troop up the steps to the bright summer sunshine.

"The air in this part of London seems cleaner than it was where we started out this morning," said Honey as they strolled down the street.

"London is a pretty gritty city," Trixie agreed.

"Grit's nothing more than a few infinitesimal, barely palpable particles of unknown substances," said Mart, well-known for his love of words.

Trixie snorted inelegantly.

"I like Trixie's version better," Jim decided. "Not only does she get right down to the nitty-gritty, but she also rhymes."

They still hadn't figured out where they were. It was a fairly quiet street, and there wasn't much traffic, so they paused on a corner.

"This has got to be the biggest city in the whole world," Trixie groaned. "My feet are killing me."

"Sixth largest," Mart said smugly. "Shanghai is number one, with eleven million people. I'd say that's just a tad bigger than Sleepyside-on-the-Hudson."

"Mart Belden, you're a human almanac!" exclaimed Honey. "I suppose you know the population of London, too?"

"I believe it's over seven million—that's if you're talking about Greater London. You have to understand that London is a city within a city," Mart explained earnestly. Not only had he found more time to read up on the trip than the others had, but he also had a phenomenal memory, much as Trixie hated to admit it sometimes.

"The oldest section in the central part is called the City of London, and it's only one square mile in area," Mart went on. "In the Middle Ages, it was walled in, like a fortress. The central part of the city, which is about ten square miles, is still the busiest section. It's surrounded by Greater London, which is around seven hundred square miles in area, including all the suburbs. But most of the sights we want to see are in the central part, on or near the banks of the Thames River: the Houses of Parliament, Westminster Abbey, the Tower of London, Buckingham Palace, St. Paul's Cathedral—even Scotland Yard!"

"If you know so much about London," Jim teased, "then tell us where we are at the moment!"

"We're on Mary-le-bone Road," Trixie said, reading haltingly off a street sign.

"That's pronounced *Mar*-li-bone," Jim said. "I've figured out how to pronounce all those long English words, like Worcestershire—that's *Woost'*rshr—and Leicester is *Lest'*r. You just come on strong with the first syllable, and swallow the rest."

Marylebone Road seemed to stretch a long way across the city map Honey was poring over. The map didn't help that much, except to confirm their gloomy suspicions that they were not headed for the Tower of London, which they had planned to see that morning.

"You must be sure to go to the Tower and see the crown jewels," Miss Trask had told them. "That will give you a place to start in tracing the necklace."

Trixie was beginning to wish that Miss Trask was spending the day with them instead of doing research. Always efficient, always a good sport, she was the Bob-Whites' favorite person to travel with. She had previously been Honey's governess but was presently the manager of the entire Wheeler estate, in which capacity she could do anything from arranging banquets to starting stalled station wagons. Besides herself, she supported her invalid sister with the salary she earned at the Wheelers'.

No one knew how old Miss Trask was. She never let on. She was attractive in a brisk, trim way, with her bright blue eyes and short, silver-gray hair. She always dressed sensibly but well, in tailored suits and sturdy shoes. Sometimes the Bob-Whites liked to tease her about a romantic interest. For example, Mr. Lytell, who ran a general store near Manor House, often seemed to feel more than just a high regard for Miss Trask. Her response to such teasing was always a calm smile that revealed absolutely nothing, and the Bob-Whites usually assumed that her busy life left no room for romance. Their private opinion was that Mr. Lytell wasn't anywhere near good enough for her. But then, who could possibly be?

Trixie had long ago decided that one of the best things about Miss Trask was that, as capable as she was, she seldom interfered with the Bob-Whites' plans or told them what to do. She seemed to give them credit for being intelligent, practical young people who could manage their own lives. Yet she was always there when they needed her. *And I think this might be a day when we'll need her*, Trixie thought to herself.

By this time, there were quite a few passersby on Marylebone Road. But the Bob-Whites were just about to give up asking directions from them.

"*Mis*directions is more like it," Trixie said plaintively. "Everything is 'just around the corner.' I really think they're all making fun of us."

" 'Pulling your leg' is the British expression, I think," Jim said.

"*Just* down at the bottom of the road, old chap," Mart said in cheery English accents. "Turn left, and keep going till you see a stytioner's shop. It's right next to the ironmonger's—*just* keep going, and there it is. You cahn't miss it."

Trixie wriggled her toes in the stout walking shoes that Miss Trask had recommended. Back home, they never wore anything on their feet for walking but sneakers—unless it was boots. This was a lot of walking, even for the active Bob-Whites, but as tired as she was, Trixie wasn't about to admit she'd had enough.

Honey caught Trixie's eye and smiled sympathetically. "Why don't we go in one of these little cafés and sit down a minute?" she asked the boys.

"You aren't by any chance intimating that the female pedal extremities are inferior to those of the male, are you?" Mart inquired with an infuriating grin.

"Not at all," Trixie retorted. "I notice you've been slowing down a bit yourself, Mr. Walking Dictionary."

"Or you could say Mr. Limping Dictionary." Jim's green eyes twinkled as he winked at Trixie, and her blue eyes sparkled back at him. She always felt so good when Jim was on her side. Of course, you couldn't expect your brother to be all that gallant. Jim was quieter than her brother, Trixie thought, but he knew a lot.

"Touché," Mart admitted with a grin. " 'A horse, a horse! My kingdom for a horse,' as the Bard would put it." The Bard, as they all knew by now, was another name for Shakespeare.

"How about a cuppa tea?" Honey persisted.

"And some of those luscious gatewks we've been seeing in the bakery windows," Trixie chimed in enthusiastically. During the previous hour, she'd been eyeing those gooey little cakes that had various kinds of icing—lemon, chocolate, fruit, butterscotch, whipped cream. They'd looked enticing.

"Gatewks?" Honey asked doubtfully.

Mart roared with laughter. "That's ga-*toe*, old girl," he informed his sister. "French for cakes. It's spelled *g-a-t-o-u-x*."

Trixie turned pink.

"You should have quit when you were ahead," Jim told Mart, with another wink at Trixie. "The correct spelling is *g-a-t-e-a-u-x*."

It was Mart's turn to blush. Spelling wasn't his strongest point. "My vocabulary is a mite better than my orthography" was all he would say. He grinned weakly and stuffed his hands in his pockets.

"Anyway, how come it's French?" Trixie asked. "I thought we were in England."

"Hey, here's Baker Street," Jim said as they came to an intersection. "And look, there's the house that's supposed to be 221-B!"

Mart unslung his camera and moved back for a better picture.

"What do you want to take a picture of that old building for?" Trixie asked. "It's just like all the others in the row."

"You claim to be a detective, and you don't know about 221-B?" her brother asked. "Let me introduce you to Sherlock Holmes, only the most famous detective ever, and that's the famous Victorian flat he and Dr. Watson are supposed to have rented. Only they didn't, of course, because they're really just fictitious characters."

"Oh, now I remember!" Trixie said excitedly.

"Look! That must be the bow window Holmes was sitting in when he got shot by his archenemy what's-his-name—" She paused, searching her memory.

"Moriarty," Honey said.

"Only Holmes didn't get killed," Trixie went on, "because he wasn't there at all! He'd left a wax dummy in the window to foil the villain."

Unfortunately, the famous flat wasn't open to tourists, as the Bob-Whites were told by a cross older woman who came to the door.

"There! You see?" Trixie said, disappointed. "They don't like us. You'd think she could at least have given us a peek."

"She didn't seem very friendly," Honey had to admit. She sighed.

"It's just the well-known British reserve," Mart said.

"Never mind, Trix," Jim told her. "We can go see Madame Tussaud's Wax Museum instead. Look—it's right around the corner."

"Gleeps," she said, cheering up in a hurry. "Let's go!"

"First we'd better fortify ourselves with a cuppa tea and some of those luscious gatewks," Jim said.

"Let's hurry up, though," Trixie said impatiently. "We still have to see Westminster Abbey and the changing of the guard at Buckingham Palace—"

"And take the cruise down the Thames," Honey added as they trooped into a small café and sat down

34

at one of the gleaming wooden tables. "And see London Bridge—"

"You can't see London Bridge," Mart said. "It's in Arizona."

"Arizona!" Trixie exclaimed. "You're kidding!"

"That's right," Jim said. "Some rich guy bought it and carted it over to Lake Havasu City in Arizona. The funny thing is—"

The funny thing about London Bridge was forgotten when a tall man in a white apron came out of the kitchen to take their orders. With his bushy moustache, he looked more than a little stern.

"Mart, you'll spoil your appetite," Honey said. "You look about ready to gobble up your menu!"

"I'm all for the British custom of eating five times a day," said Mart.

Everybody laughed—not that it was all that funny, but just because they were having a good time. They giggled even more over some of the strange-sounding foods—things like kippers and crumpets. Everything sounded so tempting.

The waiter glared down at them, and Trixie squirmed. After they'd finally made up their minds and the man had disappeared behind the swinging kitchen doors, she asked, "Why do I keep having that strange feeling that they hate us?"

"Because you're a shamus," teased Mart, "and you always have strange feelings about people you meet."

"Oh, Trix, they don't hate us," Honey said quickly.

35

"We do act sort of silly, you know—the way we make jokes about their money and the way they talk and all. And we take up so much room on their subways and buses. You can't blame someone for getting mad when he gets a subway door shut in his face."

"Honey's right," Jim said soberly.

Trixie flushed. She was born friendly. She enjoyed making new friends, and it bothered her when people weren't friendly back to her. *I guess I'm just too impulsive*, she thought to herself. *I'll probably never be as tactful and considerate of other people's feelings as Honey is. Still, I wish Jim wouldn't be so quick to side with Honey!*

"I read somewhere," Jim went on, "that there was resentment of Americans after the Second World War. The English were still on strict rations, while the American tourists could have everything they wanted and were sometimes pretty rude about getting it."

"On the other hand," Mart said, "the tourist industry is very important to their economy."

"Maybe they wish it wasn't," Honey commented wisely, just as the waiter entered with their orders.

Trixie had ordered a trifle, which was a conglomeration of pound cake, jelly, custard, fruit, and whipped cream, flavored with wine. As heavenly as it tasted, Trixie forced herself to eat a little faster than normal.

"We don't have much time," she kept reminding the others. "Miss Trask says we'll only be in London for two or three days, and we've just barely started on sight-seeing, much less on solving our case."

She grew even more impatient when they had all finished and the waiter didn't appear with their bill. They could hear dishes rattling in the kitchen, but nobody came through the swinging doors. They were the only patrons in the small café.

"Couldn't we just leave the money on the table?" she said at last.

"We could if it was dollars," Jim agreed, "but I still haven't got the hang of this English money." He took out his wallet and riffled through the pound notes, which somehow didn't look as "real" as American dollars. "These don't seem to be worth the same amount for two days in a row," he said.

Trixie fidgeted restlessly. "Could that man be keeping us waiting intentionally?" she wondered aloud.

"Ssshhh," Honey whispered as the doors finally swung open and the waiter came over to plunk their bill down on the table.

"As Winnie-the-Pooh might say, what do we owe in pounds, shillings, and ounces?" Mart asked lightly.

Pooh was a favorite of Bobby, their little brother, and Trixie felt a twinge of homesickness. Back home, everybody liked the Bob-Whites!

"Mine comes to roughly a pound, with the tip," Jim figured.

Honey unhitched the leather handbag that hung from her shoulder and stared at its contents, totally baffled by the unfamiliar money.

"Mine is ninety-five pennies," Trixie said with a sigh, rummaging around in her change purse. "Oh, woe! How am I going to come up with that many pennies?"

"That's pence," Mart told her. "Pence aren't the same thing as cents. They're worth about twice as much, and there's a hundred pence to the pound, which fluctuates around two dollars. So give the man a quid, and let him keep the change. Here, Honey, I'll pay the rest, and we can figure out how much you owe me when we get back to the hotel."

Trixie was all mixed-up, and she didn't like it. "What's a quid?" she asked.

"A quid is British slang for a pound," Mart explained patiently.

All this time, the waiter was standing there, waiting to take their money. To Trixie's mind, the face behind that moustache was scowling. Well, she didn't want to tip him too much. But maybe it wasn't enough—was that why he was glaring at her? It seemed she couldn't do anything right here.

Trixie placed her money on the table and stormed out the door, every blond curl bristling. The only possible reason that waiter could have for not liking them was that they were Americans! They hadn't done anything wrong, she was sure.

She hadn't gone far when she found Jim walking beside her. "I get that Yankee-go-home feeling, too," he admitted with a sympathetic sigh.

Trixie felt better, with Jim at her side. Maybe things would be different at the Wax Museum. Maybe they'd even start finding clues to the whole reason they were in England—the origin of Honey's necklace.

In the Chamber of Horrors • 3

As the Bob-Whites were waiting in line for admittance to the Wax Museum, an English family strolled over to stand right behind them. The small boy and girl appeared to be twins, with red hair like Jim's and blue eyes like Bobby's. They bore a closer resemblance to her little brother, Trixie thought, the way they were staring at her. She did feel a bit self-conscious, suddenly, about the fact that the four Americans were dressed in identical red jackets, the ones Honey had expertly sewn for each of the Bob-Whites.

Trixie bent down to the children and gave them her friendliest smile. "I'll bet you're wondering why we're all wearing these red jackets," she said. "You see, we belong to a club called the Bob-Whites of the Glen. That's what the initials on the back of our jackets stand for. We have to earn our own money for club dues, and we have a lot of fun together. Sometimes we even get to solve exciting mysteries. Do *you* belong to a club?"

Instead of answering, the children merely giggled and retreated behind their mother's skirt.

"The twins're a bit shy, they are," said the rosy-faced Englishwoman. "That is, with stryngers they are."

Strangers! Trixie's jaw tightened. *Why, I've always been able to make friends with little kids*, she thought stubbornly.

"And we have this special club whistle," she persisted, still bending down, "for when we get into trouble." Without stopping to think, she let out her most ear-piercing *bob, bob-white!*

With a delighted grin, the children peeked out from behind their mother. The rest of the crowd, however, backed off, and a man in uniform appeared from inside the museum.

" 'Ere now," the man said sternly. "None of that!"

Trixie hastily stood up, an uncomfortable redness spreading across her face. "I was only—" she began.

Without waiting for her to finish, the museum guard shook a warning finger at her and hurried back into the building.

"That's lucky for you," Mart murmured in Trixie's

ear. "I have a feeling your explanation would have got you into even more hot water."

"Come on, you two," Honey said peaceably. "We can go in now."

Once inside, the Bob-Whites grew quiet as they gazed at the wax figures, which wore real clothes and seemed human right down to their hair, eyelashes, and bright, sparkling eyes. The figures looked so incredibly real and so familiar that the Bob-Whites didn't even have to read their names.

"It's like seeing everybody you ever heard of, all in one place," Honey marveled. "Napoleon and the Beatles, Abraham Lincoln and Liza Minnelli, all standing around together, big as life!"

"And Shakespeare," Mart said, going over for a closer look. He consulted his guidebook. "It says here that they make an impression of the skull in wax—using the actual head, if possible. If not, an artist sculpts it. Then they stick the hairs in the warm wax, one by one. The eyes are hand-blown glass, each one perfectly color-matched to the victim—that is, uh, the subject. There's a collection of eyes in the storeroom drawers—that I have to see!"

"I've heard that many world leaders—even kings and queens—come right here to Madame Tussaud's to be measured and photographed," Jim said.

"There's Madame Tussaud in the flesh—I mean, in the wax." Trixie pointed to the famous old lady in the entrance hall. "Is she still alive?"

"Not quite." Mart grinned. "According to the guidebook, she started making wax figures way back before the French Revolution, when she was only eighteen, and she died in 1850, at the age of eighty-nine."

"It says here she modeled old Ben Franklin when he was in Paris in 1783," Jim read from the guidebook. "He was the first American statesman ever to be done in wax."

"She also did Marie Antoinette—fresh from the guillotine," Mart said. "They brought her the head in a basket." He drew a grisly line across his throat.

"Yipes," Trixie said, and she saw Honey shiver. Trixie was reminded of how Honey used to faint at the sight of blood when she first came to Sleepyside. *Now she's as determined as I am to become a detective*, Trixie thought. *Of course, she still does get scared sometimes, but that's because she tends to have more sense than I do.*

Trixie wasn't really careless. On second thought, she was always the first to agree that she had been too impulsive. The trouble was, she didn't always have her second thoughts until too late.

Thinking about Honey's early days in Sleepyside made Trixie think of the absent Bob-Whites and how much she wished they could have come. "Especially Dan—he really deserves a trip like this," Trixie said out loud, without realizing that nobody would know what she'd been thinking about. "Because he works so hard all the time!" Embarrassed, she blushed.

Honey smiled understandingly. "I wish Dan could have come, too," she said. "And Brian. They're just so serious about earning money."

"And Di's always having to go someplace with her parents," Mart said grumpily. He kind of liked Di. Unlike Trixie, she always appreciated him.

"It's probably just as well everybody couldn't come," Jim pointed out. "That would be three more people to confuse waiters and museum guards!"

Mart unslung his camera and called the others over to pose in front of a group of American presidents.

"You should be in this one," Trixie told him. "Here—let me take it."

Everybody groaned.

"Trix, you always jiggle the camera while you're taking the picture," protested Mart.

"Or else you chop off everyone's head," teased Honey. "And I've already had enough head-chopping for one day!"

Finally Jim volunteered to take the picture.

"Boy, will our history teachers be impressed," exulted Trixie. "Here we are in a picture with George Washington and Teddy Roosevelt—isn't he neat? And look—President Kennedy and Jimmy Carter. Gleeps!"

"Here's Henry the Eighth," Jim said as they walked into another hall. The bulky king was surrounded by all six of his wives.

"Talk about head-chopping!" said Mart. "That's how a few of his wives met their end, you know."

" 'E was a 'oly terror, 'e was," their mother told the little redheaded twins, who were still close behind the Bob-Whites. "A naughty man, indeed!"

Fortunately, Honey wasn't around to hear this bloodthirsty conversation. "Trixie!" she shrieked from across the room. "Come here! Here's Queen Elizabeth, and just look at her necklace. Isn't it a lot like mine? Like my inheritance?" Honey was acting so excited that the other Bob-Whites hurried over to join her immediately.

"Come now. Queue up, queue up," a stout Englishman reminded them, flourishing his skinny black umbrella. A crowd of sightseers had just surged into the Hall of Kings, and the Bob-Whites were out of line. To the British, it seemed, this was a crime second only to first-degree murder.

Honey didn't budge. She couldn't take her eyes off the red-haired queen, and Queen Elizabeth the First stared back at her disdainfully. She was wearing a glittering, bejeweled gown—and an ornate necklace of multicolored gems.

"They're not exactly like yours, though, Honey," Trixie said.

"No, but I think it proves what the appraiser told Mother," Honey insisted.

The Bob-Whites dropped behind to let the other tourists move ahead of them.

"Honey, you may be right," Jim said thoughtfully. "The appraiser said it dates back to about 1600, didn't he? That would be about the end of Queen Elizabeth's reign, wouldn't it?"

"Elizabeth the First, 1558 to 1603," Mart recited glibly.

"Elementary, my dear Watson," Trixie scoffed. "You read it off the plaque."

"I promise this is the last time I'll mention beheading," said Mart, "but I just can't resist mentioning that even Elizabeth was a decapitator. She was responsible for the beheading of Mary Queen of Scots—her own cousin!"

Jim shook his head. "I've always heard Miss Trask say how soothing she finds the sound of the Scottish accent, and I think it's neat, too. But I must say there's a lot of blood in Scottish history."

"In English history, too," said Honey with a shudder. "Come on, let's go see the Sleeping Beauty upstairs."

Trixie was only too happy to follow. The sight of another figure near Elizabeth's had slightly unnerved her. For some reason, she felt like getting as far away as possible from the bony, scar-faced figure, dressed all in gray from his battered golf cap to his dirty trousers.

Upstairs, in the shadowy Chamber of the Tableaux, lay the famous fairy-tale princess. Her long golden hair, just the color of Honey's, spilled over a white lace pillow, and her chest rose and fell as if she were alive.

"She's *breathing*," Honey whispered.

The group was also impressed by the deafening Battle of Trafalgar, laid out on two levels below. It was like a real battle at sea, with cannons roaring, smoke billowing, flares bursting, and fifty wax sailors fighting across the pitching deck of the ship.

"Wow!" said Mart. "Wonder how they build *this*."

"They do a lot with electronics," Jim explained. "Strobe lights, magnetic tape—I guess it's a lot noisier than it used to be when Madame Tussaud was around."

"Let's not forget to see the Chamber of Horrors," said Trixie. Eager to view some of history's most notorious criminals and villains, she led the way down the winding stone steps to the dungeons.

In the gloomy light, it was hard to see very well. Eerily highlighted were the faces of people like Jack the Ripper, Nazi war criminals, Lee Harvey Oswald, and a mob of French peasants gleefully watching the very guillotine that had been used in the French Revolution. Weird music drifted through the dark cells.

"Brrr," Honey shivered. "It's cold down here."

Most of the archcriminals were behind bars. "Visitors have been known to break off wax fingers for souvenirs," said Mart. "And speaking of wax fingers, I'm not leaving till I see how they put these things together. I bet we could get them to let us see the workshops."

"Go ahead," Trixie said. "I'd rather see the rest of the Horrors. How about you, Honey?"

"We-ell," Honey said, "neither alternative sounds all that attractive to me. But I guess the workshops do sound even gorier than this, so I'll stay down here."

"You go with Mart if you want to, Jim," Trixie said. "We can meet at the exit."

"I don't think we should split up," Jim said doubtfully. He glanced at Trixie.

"Oh, pish!" Trixie tossed her curls. "What could happen? All these figures are wax, remember? This must be one of the safest places in the whole world, as bloodcurdling as it looks!"

Jim grinned and looked at his watch. "Well, okay," he agreed. "But let's meet at the main exit in ten minutes. We have to find our way back to the hotel before Miss Trask decides to call in Scotland Yard."

"Only ten minutes?" Mart sighed. "Ah, 'the time is out of joint,' as the Bard would say."

"Only when you're wasting it," Trixie said pointedly, and the boys took off.

It was near teatime, and not many tourists were left in the subterranean vaults. Trixie and Honey stuck close together as they wandered from one Horror to the next.

"I'm beginning to wish I'd gone with the boys," quavered Honey.

"Just another minute," begged Trixie. "If we're going to be detectives, we have to know what we may be up against some—oh, my goodness!"

In turning a corner in a narrow passageway, Trixie had brushed against a rigid figure standing in a shadowed niche in the wall. "Look—isn't he strange?" she muttered.

Honey inched closer and, without a word, clutched Trixie's arm.

The strangest thing about him, thought Trixie, was that he looked almost exactly like that bony gray figure she'd seen up in the Hall of Kings. For a moment, the thought crossed her mind that the museum had "planted" these spooky figures in various places, as a practical joke to scare the tourists. *No, that doesn't make any sense*, she thought, moving back a step. *This has to be the same one I saw upstairs.* His pallid face was set in the same evil leer, his beady black eyes sparkled with the same brilliance, and he was dressed in the same dirty gray clothes.

"Wonder what kind of criminal he is," breathed Honey.

Trixie snapped her fingers. "A pickpocket, I bet!" Miss Trask had warned them about pickpockets in London, and this was exactly Trixie's idea of what a pickpocket would look like. She looked around for a plaque identifying this figure, but could find none.

"Come on, Trixie," Honey pleaded. "Let's get out of here."

"Wait a second." Trixie gazed steadily into the man's beady eyes, until—she was almost certain—the pale white eyelids twitched. Defiantly, she kept on staring.

"He looks so *real*," Honey whispered.

"Guess what," Trixie said grimly as the eyes wavered. "He is!"

The stiff figure broke into motion and grabbed at Honey's arm.

"Hang on to your bag!" Trixie yelled.

The little man tried to wrench the handbag from Honey, who screamed as the leather strap bit into her shoulder.

Trixie tried to pull him away, but he was surprisingly strong. His bony hands felt like steel claws as he grappled with them in the dim passageway.

Bob, bob-white! Trixie whistled shrilly.

But the boys were nowhere near.

Clues in the Catalog •4

'ERE NOW, wot's all this?''

Trixie's whistle had instantly produced a guard, probably her old friend from the entrance, although she wasn't sure.

"Quick, catch him!" Trixie urged. "He's getting away!"

"Catch 'oo?" the guard asked, looking around.

The little gray man was nowhere in sight. He had wriggled out of Trixie's clutches like a slippery fish and taken off down the dim passageway.

"Oh, Honey," she wailed. "Did he get your bag?"

"No, I—I hung on to it," Honey said, still shaking.

"Why don't you go after that pickpocket?" Trixie

demanded angrily of the guard.

The guard just stared at her.

"There! He was standing right there." Trixie pointed forcefully at the niche in the wall. "We thought he was a wax man at first, because he looked so awful, like a famous criminal. Only he wasn't wax—he was *alive*." Trixie was talking as fast as she could, so that the guard would still have time to catch the pickpocket. "Oh, please, hurry!"

The guard frowned. "Young lydy," he said, "I cahn't myke out a word you're sying, but I will 'ave to arsk you to leave. This is the second time you 'ave cre-yted a disturbance."

"You—you're throwing *me* out?" Trixie gasped, incredulous. She stared at the guard.

Honey squeezed her hand. "We'd better go."

Trixie bristled all the way back to the hotel. Fortunately, the Bob-Whites were given very good directions by a policeman, or bobby, as the English called their police.

Miss Trask was waiting for them. She showed a slight flicker of a smile when she heard how Trixie had got herself and Honey evicted from the museum, but she grew serious when the talk turned to pickpockets. "From now on, I think you should all stick together, at least while we're in London," she said. "And why doesn't everyone give me their passports? We'll leave them in the hotel safe, just in case we run into any more pickpockets."

When the Bob-Whites awoke on the following day, a Saturday, it was raining.

"It seems to rain a lot in England," commented Honey.

"Nobody pays any attention, though," Trixie said, yawning. "They carry umbrellas just as naturally as they wear shoes."

"Brollies, they call them," Mart put in.

They and Miss Trask were planning to spend the morning at the British Museum and Library, following up on the research already begun by Miss Trask. At the museum entrance, they not only had to get special reading passes but also had to be searched for bombs.

"London has survived more bombs than any great city in the world," Miss Trask told them, "mostly in the Second World War, but even today they have to keep a close watch for terrorists. In the forties, squadrons of Nazi planes flew over every day, destroying or damaging about eighty percent of the houses in London." Miss Trask's kind blue eyes clouded over as she told them about England's terrible ordeal.

"I guess there wouldn't be any London," Trixie said, "if our country hadn't entered the war."

"I don't know about that," Miss Trask demurred. "The people of Great Britain were very brave. They fought without us for over two years, and then they continued to fight beside us."

"Thank goodness this museum isn't much like the Wax Museum," Honey said as the group walked through the large exhibit halls toward the reading rooms.

Gigantic black sphinxes and bas-reliefs from ancient Egypt towered over them. There were huge marble columns from the Parthenon and almost an entire Greek temple in one of the halls.

"The purpose of this museum is a little different, too," said Miss Trask. "It's designed to preserve and interpret the history of humanity, specializing in the history of ancient and medieval civilizations. Many individuals have donated their entire collections of objects and information, making this one of the most famous museums in the world."

"Sounds like the Bob-Whites," Jim said with a grin. Whenever the Bob-Whites got a reward for solving a mystery or capturing some criminals, or whenever they found something valuable, they always gave it to someone who needed it more than they did. In fact, that was the secret purpose of their club—to help people.

"And the British Library is one of the largest libraries in the world," Miss Trask went on. "It has about eight million books. We could spend our whole lives just in the British Museum and never run out of fascinating new exhibits," she added regretfully. "But we have only ten days to find out about Honey's necklace and Mrs. Wheeler's ancestors."

"Research is fun, though," Jim said. "Even if it is hard work."

"It's just like solving a mystery," said Trixie as Miss Trask showed them how to use the library's card catalogs and reference books. "One clue leads to another! You find a card that leads you to a book, and that book leads you to another book or maybe an old map or an exhibit."

Trixie, working on Elizabethan jewelry, was not as successful in her morning's work as was Honey, who researched her ancestors, the Harts. Honey shared some of her findings during the lunch break in the museum cafeteria, which looked just like any ordinary American cafeteria with very reasonable prices and good food.

"Did any of you ever hear of Nancy Hart?" she asked.

"I believe she was a heroine of the American Revolution," Miss Trask said. "Didn't she live in Georgia?"

"Yes, and she had this famous ride, like Paul Revere's. The road she galloped down is still called the Nancy Hart Highway," Honey said. "She dressed up like a man—which was easy enough for her to do, since she was six feet tall! Then she made this log raft, tied together with honeysuckle vines, to sneak into the British camp to spy on them. Hart County and the town of Hartwell and a lot of other places were named after her." Honey's hazel eyes were glowing.

"Imagine me being descended from a Revolutionary spy!"

"Maybe." Miss Trask smiled. "Of course, she could be in another branch of your family."

"How come we had to come to the British Museum to find *that* out?" Trixie asked. "I thought your mother's ancestors lived in England."

"Well, they did," Honey said. "Just as Mother said, the tradition is that we're descended from the Shakespeare family—through his sister Joan, who married William Hart. But even so, there are still descendants in the United States, Canada, and Australia, too."

"Our Honey, practically kissin' kinswoman to the kaleidoscopic keystone of all literature!" Mart was so impressed that he almost choked on his milk.

"Oh, Mart, I think you're exaggerating," giggled Honey, pounding him on the back.

"I think we should go right on to Stratford-on-Avon," said Miss Trask. "That's where the Shakespeares lived. The homes of the poet's father and mother are both nearby, and the house he was born in, as well as his grave, are still right there in Stratford. After four hundred years, they haven't been changed. The whole town is full of Shakespearean memorabilia."

"Stratford-on-Avon—that reminds me of Sleepyside-on-the-Hudson," Trixie said, starting to feel a bit homesick again.

"Shakespearean memorabilia," Jim repeated. "Sounds like it's right up Mart's alley!"

"Alley?" huffed Mart with renewed composure. "I may have a few eight-lane superhighway cloverleafs perhaps, but no alleys!"

"I always suspected that you were born with green matter where your gray matter should be," Trixie put in.

"Well, at least there's a method to *my* madness," said Mart.

It was settled that they would make the trip on Monday. "That will give you folks a chance to see a little more of London tomorrow," Miss Trask said. "And I can finish up the research."

"But don't you want to see the sights?" Honey asked.

"Oh, I've been to London before," Miss Trask assured them.

Trixie suddenly realized that there were a lot of things about the former governess that they didn't know. She tried expressing that to the others as they left the museum later in the afternoon. Miss Trask was staying behind to do some more work. No one seemed interested in Trixie's remark.

"I'm just grateful that we have such a nice, everyday kind of person to travel with," Honey said.

Jim nodded absently, watching as Mart buttonholed a tall black man in a purple robe and red turban on the museum steps.

"Wouldn't you know?" Jim's green eyes twinkled. "People of all nationalities visit this center of learning, and Mart seems to want to talk to them all."

Trixie looked around at young German scholars with denim knapsacks; Hindu women in turquoise or lemon-colored silk saris; smiling, bespectacled Japanese and Chinese students; white-collared clergymen and midiskirted nuns; and chattering French teenagers. All were streaming in and out of the huge gray buildings.

Then Trixie caught sight of a more familiar figure, lurking behind the pillar at the iron gate.

"There! There he is!" She pointed wildly. "That little creep—in the gray cap—"

"Where?" Honey and Jim both looked, but the pickpocket had already slithered into the crowd.

"Are you sure it was him?" Honey asked.

"Sure, I'm sure," Trixie cried. "He must be following us!"

"But why would he do that?" Honey asked with a little shiver.

Trixie thought for a moment. "Well, don't you remember how I told you that I'm almost sure I saw him in the Hall of Kings, when you were showing us the Queen's necklace?" Trixie spoke slowly, figuring it out as she went along. "And we were talking really loud about your necklace. And then he went for your bag down in the Chamber of Horrors. . . ."

"But it wasn't in my handbag," Honey protested.

She looked anxiously about.

"He wouldn't know that," Trixie pointed out. "And besides," she whispered, "it is today!" They had taken it along with them to compare it with the exhibits of Elizabethan jewelry in the museum.

"Maybe we'd better—" Jim was starting to say, when Mart sauntered over.

"Well," Mart said, "let's go. My African friend says we should take a bus instead of the tube. He says you can see a lot of London from the top deck."

"Great idea," Jim agreed. "We'll get away from that pickpocket, too."

"I'm sure he's following us," Trixie muttered stubbornly as they climbed the narrow winding steps of a swaying double-decker. According to a sign on the big red omnibus, it was going to Piccadilly Circus.

"A circus!" Honey said. "That sounds like fun. We can get off there."

"Circus is a British expression for a circular area where streets intersect," Jim told her. "They have a lot of circles and squares, with monuments or parks, in London."

"Unequivocally speaking," Mart spouted happily, "Piccadilly Circus is a circumbendibus plaza near the point that is approximately equidistant from the extremities of the city."

A young English girl leaned toward them, looking puzzled but friendly. "Piccadilly's the next stop," she said helpfully.

"Oh, how do we stop the bus?" Honey asked.

The girl pointed to a sign which read, STRIP ONCE IN ADVANCE.

"Strip once in advance?" The Bob-Whites were so baffled that the girl pulled the cord for them, grinning broadly, and they all burst out laughing together.

"English and American are two whole different languages, sometimes," Mart said.

The circular plaza turned out to be not only the center of London, as Mart had said, but also its center of activity. The Americans hopped off the bus and stared goggle-eyed at the rushing traffic that swirled around the central statue, and at the sidewalks that were packed with shoppers.

"It reminds me of Times Square in New York," Trixie said. "I bet it's really lit up here at night, with all those neon signs."

Big red buses, along with bicycles, vans, and toy-sized foreign cars, clogged the street. Long-haired youths lounged on the steps of the gilded statue of Eros, the god of love, at the center of Piccadilly Circus. The morning rain had ended, and the glass storefronts were sparkling.

"Hey, that would be a neat place to eat," Mart said. "Across the street— The Carvery. I read about it in my gourmet guidebook. They have all kinds of roasts—prime rib, pork, leg of lamb, cold cuts—and you get to carve them yourself. You can eat all you want." He eyed the building hungrily.

"It is just about time to eat," Trixie agreed. "But I wanted to go to a pub. And there's a place called Tiddy Dol's. I'm just dying to go there. And—"

"There are restaurants here with food from every country in the world," Jim said. "Japan, Armenia, Portugal, Greece—you name it. I'd like to try 'em all."

"But there's one big advantage to The Carvery," Mart pointed out. "It's right across the street."

"*I'm* not going to cross *that* street," Honey said firmly.

When the Bob-Whites had sent off their first postcards that morning, Mart had written Di that English food was not as terrible as people said; it was *nectareously ambrosial*, underlined three times. Trixie had written Dan about the pickpocket. And Honey's card had read: "Dear Brian, The streets are very narrow and *wind*-y. The cars *whiz* by on the wrong side of the street, and we (Americans) are *terrified* of crossing. The pedestrian has absolutely *no* rights in this country. Wish you were here, Honey."

Mart showed Honey a black-and-white-striped crossing halfway around the circle. "They call 'em zebra crossings," he said.

"I don't know," said Honey. "Even if we cross with the light, it always seems like as soon as the light changes, the cars shoot forward as if they're out to get you. And I'm not used to the direction of the traffic, so I always look the wrong way before I cross. I think it's a national sport—going after pedestrians!"

"Come on," said Trixie, linking arms with Honey. "We'll all stick together. Concentrate on the good food awaiting us at The Carvery."

"Oh, woe," said Honey with a resigned nod.

Hundreds of sightseers and shoppers milled around the Bob-Whites as they waited for the light to change. Finally it did, and Trixie stepped off the curb. Despite their best efforts, the Bob-Whites found themselves getting separated from each other. Trixie felt Honey's arm slip from hers, but it was a few seconds before she was able to reach backward for Honey's hand.

Then she saw that somehow, Honey had been shoved off the curb. Trixie plunged desperately after her, but it seemed like a hundred arms held her back. She could hardly move, and a huge red double-decker was lumbering straight toward Honey!

"Honey, watch out!" Trixie shrieked.

Piccadilly Circus • 5

STOP!'' Trixie screamed, but of course the bus driver couldn't hear her over the din of the heavy traffic. He drove on, directly over the spot where Trixie had seen Honey.

Trixie screamed again and waved her arms frantically as she was carried along by the crowd to the opposite side of the street. Jim and Mart plowed their way through the crowd to Trixie.

"Where's Honey?" they asked anxiously.

"She's—she—" Trixie couldn't get the words out. Her hands shook, and she felt sick with dread. She pointed at the back of the bus. It was still moving.

A crowd of curious sightseers had gathered.

"I saw 'er. She went right under the bus, she did!"

"Och, the poor lass!"

A ripple of horror ran through the onlookers.

"But where *is* she?" Jim demanded, starting to head back across the street.

A second bus was passing, close behind the first, but still there was no sign of Honey.

"There!" Mart cried. "There she is!"

A tall man with grizzled black hair was pushing his way toward them, with Honey in his arms. Her long blond hair hung over his shoulder. When he reached the Bob-Whites, he set her down—limp and pale, but all in one piece.

"Oh, Honey!" Trixie burst into tears.

"I'm okay," Honey said shakily. "This m-man saved my life."

The big man reddened at their chorus of thank-you's. "My pleasure," he said gruffly. Then he introduced himself as Gordie McDuff. He was about Miss Trask's age, Trixie thought, and very good-looking, with his dark wavy hair and graying sideburns. He looked to be over six feet tall.

The Bob-Whites invited him to have dinner with them at The Carvery. "We just have to thank you for saving Honey's life," they insisted.

"Then ye have returned the favor already," he laughed. "For now ye have saved my life."

What does he mean by that? Trixie wondered, but before she could ask, they were heading into the restaurant and prowling around the horseshoe-shaped buffet. When it came time to carve mouth-watering slices of the sizzling-hot roast meats, McDuff proved to be an expert carver. Honey had recovered enough to show her own skill at carving, and Trixie did nearly as well.

After they returned to their table with heaped plates, the Scotsman explained his earlier remark.

"I'm in something of a predicament," he said. "I wouldna have dreamed I'd be eating a fine dinner this night—with nary a quid in me pocket." He went on to tell how he had just arrived from Canada that afternoon, after the Exchanges had closed, and he had been unable to get his money changed. It was fortunate that he had met such kind people.

"But where will you sleep?" Honey asked worriedly. "What will you do tomorrow? It's Sunday! Here—"

She unslung her handbag and was about to open it, when Trixie stopped her with a look that said, *Your necklace is in there.*

"Here's five pounds," Trixie said quickly, opening her own wallet. "Would that be enough to tide you over?" She hoped so; it was all she had.

Honey read the warning flash in Trixie's eyes and was silent. She looked bewildered, though. Could Trixie be suspicious of the man who had saved her life?

"That's very kind of ye." McDuff didn't hesitate

about taking the money. "Ye may be sure I will return it," he promised with a dramatic roll of his *r*'s. "As soon as the Exchanges open on Monday. Now, if ye would just give me the name of yer hotel?" He drew out paper and pencil and waited expectantly.

Trixie was about to tell him that he didn't have to bother repaying her, when Honey spoke up.

"We're staying at a small bed-and-breakfast place—the Garden Hotel—near the British Museum, but we're leaving on Monday," she confided. "You really don't have to return the money. My parents will be glad to give it to Trixie. But we'd just love to have you meet Miss Trask—our chaperon—and have lunch with us tomorrow." She finished her speech in a rush, breathless and a little pink.

McDuff's black eyes twinkled. "Happen I could. If ye're certain this Miss Trask wouldna object?"

Honey gave a glowing account of her former governess, and then she and the boys told the Scotsman something about their trip. By unspoken consent, no one mentioned the necklace, although Honey seemed on the verge of it several times.

Trixie was unusually quiet. She couldn't understand why she wasn't as crazy about McDuff as the rest of them were. Even Jim seemed to be under his spell. *What's the matter with me?* she thought. *Honey wouldn't be here if it wasn't for him. She'd be in some London hospital, or maybe even*—She couldn't bear to finish the thought.

"We're on a genealogical binge," Mart was explaining as he finished up his third helping, "trying to find out something about Honey's forebears, with a modicum of sight-seeing on the side."

"That is, when we're not getting lost or falling under buses," Honey said with a laugh. She seemed to have completely gotten over her narrow escape.

"I'll never forget, sir, what you did for my sister," Jim said solemnly when they were through eating. He held out his hand.

McDuff clasped it warmly. Then he strode off, leaving the Bob-Whites to figure out how to divvy up the bill.

"Just the same," Trixie said later, after they'd recounted their adventures to Miss Trask, "there's something strange about that man."

Everybody laughed.

"Trixie Belden, you're a schlocky Sherlockian shamus. (Try saying *that* five times fast!) You couldn't exist without 'something strange' in your life. And if it's not there, you just go ahead and make it up," accused Mart.

Trixie ignored him. "And what's more," she went on, "I saw that pickpocket again today—*twice*." She glanced around the group triumphantly.

The boys looked skeptical, but Honey turned pale. "Where?" she asked.

"Once in front of the British Museum, like I told you, and again—" Trixie paused mysteriously—"in

Piccadilly Circus. *Right before you got pushed off that curb.*"

"Like I said, if it's not there, you make it up. Now you're going to see Gray Cap everywhere we go," Mart hooted.

"But, Mart, I do," Trixie insisted. "I'm developing my powers of observation."

"Your powers of *imagination* are incomparable," conceded her brother.

"Sounds like it's time for bed," Miss Trask said diplomatically.

Early the following morning, the Bob-Whites were on their way to the Sunday morning services at Westminster Abbey. Miss Trask had said she had a slight headache, and so she was sleeping in.

"It's all the studying." Trixie wrinkled her freckled nose. Research was more fun than she had expected, but she wouldn't want to do it all day. Miss Trask, however, seemed never to tire of it.

"Trix, about that pickpocket," said Jim. "You know, it could be that you're seeing different ones. Everybody's been warning us that London is full of them."

"And they would all dress sort of like that," Honey put in. "I mean, all in gray, so no one would notice them."

"Inconspicuous," Jim agreed.

"Delitescent," Mart tossed off nonchalantly.

"Where?" Trixie looked up and down the shop-lined street. "I didn't know they had any."

"Had any what?" Mart's blue eyes were as puzzled as his sister's.

"Delicatessens, silly. And anyhow, I don't see how you could be hungry already, after that super breakfast we had at the hotel."

Mart chortled. "I wasn't talking about salamis, sibling. I said *delitescent*."

"You got me," Jim said.

"Delitescent—it means lying hidden," said Mart. "Any self-respecting private investigator ought to know that."

"And we know *you* well enough," Trixie said with a toss of her curls, "to safely assume that you'd be talking about food, not detective terms."

Westminster Abbey turned out to be a magnificent cathedral, its massive stone buttresses black with age. Inside, the Bob-Whites gasped at the beauty of the gold-screened altar and stained-glass windows. The Abbey Choir sounded like a band of angels.

After the service, the four friends walked around, looking at the engraved stones and gilded statues that lined the walls. Plaques in the floor, too, commemorated England's famous dead. Some of the tombs were centuries old, some quite recent. Many of the names carved on them were familiar to the Bob-Whites from their classes at school.

"It's sort of like a cemetery right inside a church,"

Honey said. "I read where being buried here is practically the greatest honor England can give to someone."

"Hey, here's Chaucer," Mart cried as they wandered into the Poet's Corner.

Trixie shivered at the thought of the bones of poets she studied in school being buried right under her feet. "Jeepers," she whispered, "I'm walking on T. S. Eliot!"

There were famous scientists, too, like Sir Isaac Newton, and musicians, artists, and statesmen.

After Westminster Abbey, the Bob-Whites took in the nearby Houses of Parliament, with the famous clock in the tower.

"Big Ben got hit by a bomb during the war and went right on ticking," Mart recalled from his reading.

"Speaking of clocks, I think it's time we go back to the hotel," said Trixie. "Miss Trask was sure she'd feel up to going to the Tower of London by now."

Their chaperon certainly had recovered, the Bob-Whites found out when they returned. She was sitting in the little flower garden behind the small hotel— with Gordie McDuff. They looked as if they'd been sitting there for some time and were old friends already.

"Mr. McDuff has offered to show us around the Tower," she told the Bob-Whites. "He was a tour guide before he emigrated to Canada." Her cheeks were pink, and her bright blue eyes were sparkling.

"Doesn't she look pretty?" Honey whispered in Trixie's ear.

Trixie was too full of confusing emotions to respond. She wasn't sure she *wanted* Miss Trask to look pretty.

The Tower of London turned out to be twenty-one towers surrounded by thick walls and a moat. McDuff peppered the conversation with a multitude of names, dates, and interesting facts.

"This group of buildings is strong enough to hold off an army," he explained as he led the Bob-Whites and Miss Trask into the grassy space between the many towers that ringed the oldest tower. "Yon's the White Tower. It was built by William the Conqueror, after the Battle of Hastings in 1066." Trixie stared, awed by its age and history.

"That's one of the three dates I can ever remember," Honey confessed. "That and 1492 and 1776."

Mart, for once, was all ears and no mouth as he kept busy taking notes. "Filling up my think tank," he admitted cheerfully when the others teased him about his silence.

Miss Trask, too, was quieter than Trixie would have expected. She'd always thought that Miss Trask knew a lot about history. Perhaps Miss Trask was thinking, as Trixie was starting to admit, that McDuff made an excellent guide.

"In 1215, the Tower was held by the citizens of London in ransom for the completion of the Magna Carta," McDuff went on.

"The Magna Carta!" Jim was impressed. "That's the foundation of English law—and liberty."

"American independence, too," Mart said. "The rights of the people."

"But I thought they always had kings and queens in England," said Honey.

"Seems like they were always chopping off people's heads, too," Trixie commented.

McDuff threw back his grizzled black head and laughed. "Ye're right, little girl," he told her, "as ye all will see when we visit the Bloody Tower, where they found the bones of the two little princes who were killed by their wicked uncle. We'll also see the site of the scaffold where some of Henry the Eighth's wives and Lady Jane Grey were beheaded. But from the time of the Magna Carta to this very day, the English people have had a say in their government."

"Many of the rights the citizenry fought for in 1215 were included in the Bill of Rights attached to our own Constitution," Miss Trask added, smiling at McDuff.

Trixie was still smarting from being called a "little girl," when one of the big black birds on the Tower Green took a peck at her leg.

"Yipes!" she cried indignantly. "He bit me!"

"You're too much of a temptation," gibed Mart,

"what with all the gateaux and trifles you've been consuming."

Trixie was about to begin a hot retort when McDuff spoke up. "That's one of the Tower Ravens, a protected species. There's an ancient saying that when the last raven flies away, the Tower will fall. So to make sure they don't," he added, "their wings have been clipped."

"Hmph," Trixie sniffed. "I wish they'd consider clipping their beaks."

There was so much to see: the ruins of the Lion Tower, so called because it was once a London zoo; the living quarters of many famous prisoners, and the messages they scratched on the ancient stone walls before they were led out to execution; the collections of weapons and medieval armor.

"Even the horses wore armor," Trixie giggled. "Imagine the Wheeler horses in these aluminum horse blankets!"

Mart groaned. "That's a coat of mail. Mail, little girl, happens to be iron—hardly aluminum, in the Middle Ages. Although," he muttered to himself, "aluminum's high reflectivity and malleability, as well as its resistance to oxidation, would make it a good choice—"

"There's an awfully long line waiting to see the crown jewels," Honey said anxiously. "What if they close before we get a chance to see if they're anything like my—"

Trixie gave her a warning nudge.

"Yes, we should go see the jewels now," Miss Trask agreed.

McDuff led the way, with Miss Trask close behind him, then the boys, and Trixie and Honey trailing behind. The long line of sightseers was making its way slowly around the roped-off entrance to the Wakefield Tower, where the fabulous jewels were displayed in a heavily guarded, circular glass case as big as a room.

"You really shouldn't talk about you-know-what in front of you-know-who," Trixie told Honey in a low voice.

"I know," Honey admitted contritely. "I just keep forgetting that Mr. McDuff isn't one of us. He's so wonderful."

"He doesn't call *you* a little girl," Trixie said stiffly. Honey was taller than she was and a lot prettier, in Trixie's opinion. She didn't mind that, but she wasn't about to be called a *child*. And it didn't help any that Mart had noticed it, too, and was teasing her by calling her the same thing.

"Honestly, Trix," Honey sighed. "I don't see how you can not like Mr. McDuff! Not when he—"

"I know. He scooped you out from under that horrible bus." Trixie put her arm around Honey's waist and gave her a big hug. "Oh, Honey, I'm so glad you're okay. And I will try to like him better." She glanced toward McDuff and sighed.

A large party of American tourists had pushed in between them and the boys. Jim caught the girls' attention and pointed at a sign that was posted on the wall.

BEWARE PICKPOCKETS, it read.

The Crown Jewels · **6**

DON'T WORRY," Trixie assured Honey. "There's plenty of beefeaters around to protect us."

They giggled at the nickname of the Tower guards, who wore bright red costumes with white ruffs, white gloves, black hats, red stockings with fancy garters, and red-and-white buckled shoes. This was the traditional uniform of the Yeomen of the Guard, McDuff had explained.

"But why beefeaters?" Trixie had wanted to know.

"Aye—well—all Englishmen are referred to as beefeaters," their Scottish guide had said with a chuckle. "I dinna why!"

"Indubitably because they ingest an inordinate

amplitude of pulverized bovine flesh," Mart had suggested.

McDuff had simply given him a puzzled stare.

Miss Trask and the boys were reaching the large chamber where the jewels were displayed, and Trixie and Honey were almost there, when Honey gave a little squeal.

"Trix!" she cried. "I thought I felt something sort of tugging at my bag."

Trixie whirled around and scanned the crowd behind them. She didn't see anyone who looked like the man they called Gray Cap.

"Maybe Gray Cap knows that we'd recognize him by now," she muttered, "and he's in disguise."

A rough bump from behind sent Trixie head over heels, and as she scrambled to her feet, she heard a shrill *bob, bob-white!*

Honey was standing there, white as a sheet. "I—I whistled," Honey said faintly.

The boys were there in a split second, but it was too late. Honey's handbag was gone!

Honey hadn't been able to turn around in time to see who took it, and none of the tourists around her were of much help.

McDuff shook his grizzled black head. "They're very clever, these pesky thieves," he said worriedly. He obviously felt somewhat responsible. "I should have taken care of ye," he kept saying. "I'll notify the police as soon as we've left the Tower."

"It's a good thing your mother sent that cablegram this morning," Trixie said to Honey as they moved on toward the crown jewels.

Mrs. Wheeler had cabled Honey to be sure to leave the necklace in the hotel safe at all times. "I've been in touch with the appraiser, and it may prove to be more valuable than we at first thought," the cable had said. The Bob-Whites knew that Honey had followed her mother's instructions, so they weren't sure why Honey still seemed so upset.

"Did you have much money with you?" Jim asked.

"No, but"—tears welled up in Honey's hazel eyes—"I—I'm afraid Mother's cable was in my handbag."

Jim gave a low whistle. "Then if Trixie's right and that fellow you saw in the Wax Museum *is* following us, now he'll have all the more reason to keep following us."

The four Bob-Whites stared at each other in dismay, and McDuff looked puzzled. "What fellow is that?" he asked Miss Trask.

"I don't believe for a minute that there's anyone following us," she said firmly. "London is notorious for pickpockets."

"No matter how many pickpockets there are," Trixie said, "it sure seems strange that they're all picking on us."

"It *is* a coincidence," Miss Trask agreed.

The two girls kept their eyes open for signs of the gray pickpocket, but all was forgotten when the Bob-

Whites passed the great glass rotunda filled with the crown jewels. There were magnificent crowns sparkling with precious gems, jeweled swords and golden spurs, scrolled bracelets and ivory scepters, purple velvet and ermine caps set with diamonds and pearls, and the huge Koh-i-noor diamond from India.

"This diamond has been worn at the coronation of three queens since Victoria," McDuff told them. "It's said to bring bad luck to a man, but good luck to a woman."

Well, it sure brought bad luck to Honey, Trixie thought. She could have looked at the jewels for another few days, but there was a long line of tourists behind her.

"I didn't see any necklaces," Honey protested as McDuff led them out of the Tower and back to their hotel.

"Ssshhh," Trixie warned her. Then she saw that she didn't need to worry. McDuff was too busy talking to Miss Trask to hear what Honey said.

Trixie overheard part of his chatter—"that's a bonny blue dress that ye are wearing"—and grimaced. She could see for herself that Miss Trask was wearing one of her sensible navy blue suits. It was attractive, of course, but not "bonny."

The upshot of his chat with Miss Trask was really something to worry about, however, at least for Trixie. After McDuff had left them at the hotel, Miss Trask turned to the Bob-Whites.

"Guess what," she said, her eyes sparkling. "Mr. McDuff has consented to be our guide for the rest of the trip. He'll hire a car and drive us to Stratford tomorrow. In case anything goes wrong with the car, he says he's an experienced mechanic, and I really wasn't looking forward to driving on the wrong side of the road. He knows a great deal about Stratford, too. Oh, children, aren't we lucky?"

Children, Trixie fumed. *She never called us that before.*

The others were delighted. "That's wonderful," Honey said.

Jim was a little surprised, he told the others later, that Miss Trask would want a chauffeur. Miss Trask had gone to bed, and their brothers had stopped in the girls' bedroom for a late-night snack.

"I mean, Miss Trask loves to drive," Jim went on, "and she's a better mechanic than just about anyone else I know."

"I've been wondering . . ." Trixie hesitated, then frowned. *I've been wondering if I should tell them what I've been wondering,* she thought. *Especially Honey, who thinks McDuff is so absolutely fantastic. And Honey is probably right. She very often is right. But still . . .*

"I bet you guys didn't know that my sister turns into a pumpkin every night around this time," Mart was saying brightly.

Trixie snapped to attention. "That's better than being a pumpkin all day long," she retorted. "What I've been wondering is, did you see the newspaper tonight?"

"Don't tell me you've been reading the newspapers!" Mart smote his freckled forehead. "On summer vacation?"

"A detective has to keep up with the press," Trixie said virtuously. "To tell the truth, I was just talking about the headline on the front page."

"Yep, I saw that," Jim said. "It was a story about this tourist racket, where these con artists get poor kindhearted suckers to lend them a couple of quid—"

"*Till the Exchange opens on Monday,*" Trixie finished triumphantly. "There! You see? That's exactly what McDuff did to us."

Honey did not agree. "Just because there *are* con men doesn't make Mr. McDuff one," she began reasonably. Then, in one of her rare displays of temper, she demanded, "Why don't you just admit that you haven't liked him right from the start, Trixie Belden? I—I'll bet you're jealous!"

"Jealous?" Trixie blazed back. "Why on earth would I be jealous?" It made her feel miserable to fight with her best friend, but she couldn't seem to stop herself. And she knew Honey must be feeling just as awful. Honey hardly ever got mad.

"Because everybody else likes him so much," Honey fumed. "That's why! And because you're afraid Miss Trask is going to m-marry him!"

81

"Marry him?" Trixie hooted. "Jeepers, Honey, she only just met him!"

Mart and Jim exchanged looks and slipped back to their room, apparently unwilling to add to the tension already brewing.

Trixie hardly noticed they were gone. Her feelings were all churned up. She was terribly ashamed of herself for getting mad in the first place, and wondering how she could possibly be mad at Honey. Honey was only being loyal, the way she was to all her friends. And McDuff was certainly being friendly to them all.

But something inside Trixie kept her going. The more she wanted to stop, the more she couldn't. And Honey seemed to be having the same problem.

"You know, Trixie," said Honey, "I was going to give that five pounds to him, but, oh, no! You were so afraid he'd catch a glimpse of my necklace. I'll pay you back your old five pounds. I'll even give you ten pounds. I happen to think that what he did was worth a lot more than that. He risked his life for me!"

All of a sudden, Trixie didn't feel angry anymore. She reached for Honey's hand. "I wouldn't trade you for a million pounds," she said, and they both burst into tears.

"Thank goodness the boys left when they did," Honey sniffed as they got into their pajamas and brushed their hair. "Oh, Trix, I just *hate* fighting."

"Me, too," Trixie said. "Especially with you."

Even with peace restored, it still took Trixie a long time to fall asleep. She couldn't seem to get rid of her suspicions. *It wasn't just the five pounds I lent him,* she was thinking. *Miss Trask gave him twenty pounds to hire us a car tomorrow!*

Trixie punched her pillow and turned it over and over. *We'll never see that man again. I'm sure of it,* she thought indignantly. At the same time, she was almost hoping he *wouldn't* show up in the morning. She didn't particularly want him along on their trip.

Of course—she pounded her pillow again—that would be an awfully expensive way to get rid of him. Maybe Honey was right. Maybe she *was* jealous. . . . No! That was utterly ridiculous. Still, she couldn't think of any other good reason not to make the effort to like the tall Scotsman. . . .

If he showed up.

The Maroon Saloon • 7

So, WHERE'S McDUFF?'' Trixie demanded, the minute Miss Trask and the Bob-Whites had finished breakfast the next morning. They were sitting at their table in the little hotel, making plans for their last day in London.

"Your manner of referring to Mr. McDuff leaves something to be desired," Miss Trask said dryly. "And as to his not being here yet, he told me not to expect him until noon. He is anxious to get his English money at the Exchange before we leave London. He wants to pay you back, Trixie. After that, he plans to go to the Auto Hire to rent us a car, and he has also kindly offered to check with the police again, con-

84

cerning Honey's handbag. He has a lot to do.''

"Oh.'' Trixie felt like a balloon that had just been pricked by a pin.

"Would that you evinced such alacrity and celerity every Monday morning," Mart teased her.

"I don't know about celery, but I am dying to get to Stratford,'' she said impatiently. "I have a hunch that's where we're going to solve the mystery of Honey's inheritance.''

"I'm with Trix,'' Honey said loyally. "And besides, the sooner we get out of this city, the better.''

"I'm glad to see you two are on speaking terms again,'' said Jim, "but I don't understand why you want to leave. We haven't seen half the sights yet.''

"Well, there's one sight I don't ever want to see again.'' Honey shuddered. "And that's that horrible pickpocket.''

"To make the best of the time we have left,'' Miss Trask suggested, "you might like to take the cruise down the Thames to Greenwich. You'll see the Houses of Parliament, the Tower and the Tower Bridge, and a great deal more of London's waterfront. Then there's the Maritime Museum at Greenwich, with models of sloops and steamers, old maps, charts, and early instruments of navigation. You can go aboard an old China tea clipper, the *Cutty Sark*, and see a fascinating collection of carved figureheads taken from wrecked ships.''

"Greenwich.'' Jim's green eyes sparkled. "Is that

where they have the prime meridian? You know—
what all the world's time zones are measured by?"

"Right," Mart said enthusiastically. "Let's go!"

"But Trixie and I wanted to do a little shopping in
London," Honey said. "We have to get some souvenirs for the folks back home, and I'm going to have
to get another handbag. Could we do that, too?"

"Shopping?" the boys asked, incredulous.

"Nobody asked you to come along," Trixie assured
them.

"There wouldn't be time for both," Miss Trask
said, "and I hate to have you split up."

"And what if you get lost again?" Jim looked a bit
worried.

"Oh, I know how to get around London now,"
Trixie said confidently. "And we won't have any-
thing pick-able in our pockets, since we're leaving
Honey's necklace here in the hotel safe."

"We don't even have very much money," Honey
added.

"Expenses" for the Belden-Wheeler Detective
Agency didn't include souvenirs. The Wheelers could
have given Honey all the spending money she asked
for, of course, but she didn't want any more than
Trixie had—which, until McDuff returned her five
pounds, was just about zilch.

"We'll be careful," Trixie promised.

"Very well," their chaperon decided.

"You're such a jolly good sport!" said Honey.

"I try," Miss Trask chuckled. "You needn't be back on the dot of twelve, by the way. When Mr. McDuff gets here with the car, we'll have to pack it. Then I think we should all have lunch before we leave. You go ahead and eat wherever you like, and then be back here before two. Mr. McDuff says it isn't far to Stratford—no more than a two-hour drive."

Hmm, thought Trixie as the two girls went outside to wait for a double-decker, *if McDuff does show up, things are certainly working out conveniently for him. He gets to have lunch with Miss Trask, just the two of them. . . .*

Usually, Trixie talked over her suspicions with Honey, but by then it was clear that Honey didn't want to hear them. The morning paper had had another headline on tourist rackets, but Trixie knew enough not to bring *that* up again.

I'm not going to say any more about it till two o'clock, Trixie resolved. *If he hasn't shown up by then, they'll have to believe me.*

"I hear the shops in London are really super," Honey said, "but I kind of wish we could have gone on the cruise, too."

"We can trade notes with the boys later," Trixie said.

The girls got off the bus in Mayfair, the fashionable shopping district Miss Trask had recommended. After they picked out a red leather handbag for Honey, they went window-shopping. Here and there, between the large department stores, were small, hole-in-the-wall stationery stores, which sold magazines, sweets, and souvenirs. Honey lent Trixie some money, and Trixie treated herself to a bag of sweets.

"This has got to be the best candy in the world," she sighed, selecting several luscious chocolate bars with gooey raspberry or orange fillings, some pieces of real English toffee in all different flavors, and a few bright-colored gumdrops that tasted much better than American gumdrops.

"It probably has the most calories, too," said Honey, not that she ever had to worry about her weight.

Trixie didn't worry either, even though people were always calling her things like "sturdy." Then she remembered that Mart sometimes called her worse things than that, and she turned away from the candy section.

"Ohhh, look!" Trixie cried. "I just have to get that for Bobby."

On a crowded shelf stood a miniature London policeman, leading a police dog on a red leash. About three inches high, he wore a dark blue uniform and a round black felt hat with a strap under his chin.

"Oh, Trix, he's darling," Honey agreed. "Look, he even has a tiny necktie."

"Bobby will flip," Trixie said. "I can't wait to tell him that English cops are called bobbies."

"Now we have to find something for Di and Brian

and Dan," Honey reminded her.

Before they found just what they wanted, Trixie noticed that it was past twelve. "Do you think we could eat at Tiddy Dol's?" she begged.

"What's this thing you have about Tiddy Dol's?" Honey asked.

"I don't know," Trixie said. "I just like the name!"

It turned out that Tiddy Dol had been an eighteenth-century gingerbread peddler, and that the specialty of Tiddy Dol's Eating House was still gingerbread. The girls ate it warm, with butter, honey, and cream, and they had so many helpings that they had to rush in order to get back to the hotel in time.

"We can go shopping again in Stratford," Trixie said as they scurried through the front door of the hotel, right on the dot of two o'clock.

Jim and Mart arrived just as they did, out of breath from running.

"Where's Miss Trask?" Honey asked. There was no sign of either her or McDuff.

"Jeepers, where could she be?" Trixie asked anxiously. "She told us to be here for sure—and now *she's* gone."

"Let's ask someone around the hotel," Jim suggested, leading the way out a side door.

Mrs. Johnson, the proprietor of the little hotel, was in the garden, picking roses. "You've no call to worry," she reassured the Bob-Whites. "The gentleman as was here yesterday came by in a car and picked her up. That was about noon, I should say."

"She went off without us?" Honey's big hazel eyes were puzzled. "Didn't she leave any message?"

"No, luv, not with me she didn't."

"O Miss Trask, Miss Trask, wherefore art thou, Miss Trask," Mart said lightly, but he, too, looked concerned.

"I told you he was a crook," Trixie wailed. "He's probably kidnapped her and is holding her for a huge ransom."

Jim and Mart burst out laughing. "Oh, come on, Trix," Jim said. "You've really gone out on a limb this time."

"They probably went somewhere for lunch," Honey said doubtfully, "and just got caught in a traffic jam or something."

"But it's almost three o'clock," Trixie said indignantly, after they had waited a while longer. "I'm going to call Scotland Yard."

Before Trixie could move from where she was sitting on the hotel steps, a dark red sedan drew up under the portico of the Garden Hotel, and McDuff got out of the driver's seat on the right side of the car. Then he walked around to open the door for Miss Trask, who, even Trixie had to admit, certainly didn't look as if she'd been kidnapped.

"I'm so sorry," Miss Trask said. "We didn't notice the time." Her short gray hair was blown every which way, and her blue eyes were shining. Her brown tweed suit was adorned with a yellow chiffon scarf that Trixie had never seen before.

The Bob-Whites couldn't believe their ears. Miss Trask, the efficient manager of the Wheeler estate—forgetting the *time?*

McDuff was peeling a five-pound note from a fat roll of bills. "Here ye are, lass," he told Trixie. "I certainly appreciated the loan."

Trixie turned bright red. *Gleeps*, she gulped silently. *I really goofed this time.* How wrong could she get? He wasn't a crook, or a con man, or a kidnapper, or even a fortune hunter, since Miss Trask didn't have a fortune. He must be what he appeared to be—their friend. *I'll just have to make it up to him*, she resolved. *From now on, I'm going to be as nice as pie. . . . Even if I don't like him all that much*, she couldn't help adding to herself.

Aloud she mumbled, "You're quite welcome."

The car McDuff had picked out for them was a four-door with just enough room for the six of them. "I wasn't sure whether ye wanted an estate or a saloon," he said.

"What do you mean, saloon?" Mart asked. They were all standing around the car, admiring it. Its bright chrome sparkled in the sunlight.

Miss Trask laughed. "Mr. McDuff says that an estate is what a station wagon is called here," she explained. "And a saloon is a sedan."

"A saloon?" giggled Honey. "I thought a saloon

was where the cowboys are always going in Western movies.''

"Got it!'' Mart snapped his fingers and ran his hand fondly over the gleaming, dark red fender. "Remember when we went to Vermont, and Di and I named our beige Volkswagen the Tan Van? Well—get this—I hereby christen this car the Maroon Saloon!''

"Oh, Mart, that's neat!'' squealed Honey.

"If Di were here,'' Trixie teased, "she'd think Mart's wit was second only to Shakespeare's.''

Mart pointed a finger and ordered, " 'Get thee to a nunnery!' ''

Instead of obeying, Trixie made a face at him and got into the car.

In a short while, the Maroon Saloon was heading north, Gordie McDuff at the wheel and Miss Trask sitting beside him. The four Bob-Whites were a little cramped in the backseat, but they didn't mind. It was a sunny day, and the countryside was greener than the emeralds in Honey's necklace. Soft white clouds sailed across an azure sky.

When McDuff's deep voice broke into a Scottish song, they all joined in:

> "Speed, bonny boat, like a bird on the wing,
> 'Onward,' the sailors cry.
> 'Carry the lad that was born to be king,
> Over the sea to Skye.'

> Loud the winds howl, loud the waves roar,
> Thunderclouds rend the air.
> Baffled our foes stand by the shore,
> Follow they will not dare."

"That song's about Bonnie Prince Charlie, right?" Mart asked.

"Now, there's a brainy laddie," said McDuff. "Aye, the Young Pretender he was called by those who didn't agree that he was the rightful king. Those people won out, too, and defeated Charles in battle at Culloden Moor."

"Did Prince Charlie escape?" Honey asked.

"He probably got his head chopped off," Trixie guessed, "like Mary Queen of Scots."

"No, no, he escaped to France," McDuff said.

Kindhearted Honey breathed a sigh of relief.

"Were you born in Scotland, Mr. McDuff?" Trixie asked politely.

"Aye, little girl, that I was. In Glasgow." McDuff's big hands swung the car easily around one of the grassy circles that punctuated the straight and narrow motorway.

"When did you move to Canada?" Trixie persisted.

"Really, Trixie," Miss Trask said, "perhaps Mr. McDuff doesn't want to tell us his life story."

"I was only trying to be friendly," Trixie mumbled.

"Ask away," laughed their guide. "I don't mind. In truth, I was but a wee lad when my father emigrated to the land of promise."

Jim smiled down at Trixie, who was squeezed in between him and Honey. "I believe you said you'd been a guide in London," he said to the Scotsman. "Then you've been here before?"

"Many times," McDuff said. "But the occasion of my present journey is a sad one, ye might say. Or ye might not, depending upon how ye look at it. This was to have been my honeymoon."

Trixie sucked in her breath. "What—what happened to your, uh, fiancée?"

McDuff threw back his grizzled black head and roared. "If it's kicking the bucket ye're worried about, lassie, don't bother. She's still in the land of the living. To tell ye the truth, I was jilted."

There was a chorus of protests. "I'm terribly sorry," said Honey.

"Dinna waste your sympathy," McDuff said. "Two can't travel for the price of one, that's what I say. And I've surely fallen into good company on my road to Scotland. 'Oh, you'll take the high road, and I'll take the low road, and I'll be in Scotland afore ye,' " he sang, and they all joined in. " 'But I and my true love will never meet again, on the bonny, bonny banks of Loch Lomond.' "

He sure doesn't act like his heart is broken, thought Trixie.

Aloud she inquired, "Then you're on your way to Scotland now?"

"Aye, to visit my uncle. But there's no great rush,"

McDuff assured them. "I'll be glad to be your guide for a few days."

Mart, unusually quiet so far, was sitting by the window, looking out at the countryside. Rolling green hills, wooded estates, and stone-walled villages flashed by. Then pastures and ancient brick farmhouses became more frequent.

"Jeepers," Mart said. "These farmers use trees for windbreaks, and piles of stones or hedges instead of fences. Those must be what they call hedgerows—how about that? And look at all the sheep!"

"Mart plans to major in agriculture when he goes to college," Trixie explained to McDuff, still trying her best to be friendly. "Back home, we live on a farm, but it's just a small one, and my dad works in a bank, so we don't raise crops exactly—except raspberries and crab apples, of course—but anyway, Mart is planning to teach at Jim's school for underprivileged boys, and—"

"Whoa!" Mart pleaded. "Pipe down, will you? I'd like to find out something about English farming."

"Happy to oblige," said McDuff. "These are the Cotswold Hills—hilly, upland territory and sheep country. The pastures are laid out in neat rectangles and bounded—as ye noticed, lad—by hedges and rows of trees."

Mart's blue eyes were filled with admiration at the notion of fences that one planted.

"We learned a whole lot about sheep on my

Uncle Andrew's farm in Iowa," Trixie told McDuff.

McDuff didn't seem to hear her. "I love the English countryside," he was telling Miss Trask, "even better than London."

"It's so peaceful," Honey agreed happily. "No pickpockets!"

Trixie was about ready to give up on conversation altogether, when she looked out the window and noticed a road sign. "Stow-on-the-Wold," she laughed. "What's that?"

"I believe it's one of England's little hamlets," Miss Trask said.

"Hamlet? I thought England had only one—the play by Shakespeare," Trixie said.

"The word also means a village," said Miss Trask without turning around.

Trixie slouched down in the seat. *Either I've turned totally paranoid*, she thought, *or there is a let's-see-how-dumb-we-can-make-Trixie-look plot afoot.* She saw McDuff glance over to smile at Miss Trask, and without thinking, she muttered out loud, "He could at least keep his eyes on the road."

Mart overheard her and raised an eyebrow. "Lord, what fools these detectives be," he misquoted pointedly.

"What's that you said?" Miss Trask turned around. "Quoting Shakespeare again? How appropriate—Mr. McDuff says we're coming into Shakespeare country." She smiled at Mart.

"Just a little paraphrasing from *A Midsummer Night's Dream*," said Mart nonchalantly.

A midsummer nightmare *is more like it*, Trixie thought gloomily.

The Tweedies · 8

TRIXIE'S HIGH SPIRITS began returning, bit by bit, as the Maroon Saloon entered Stratford.

"Gleeps!" she whispered. "Isn't this marvelous?"

They were driving slowly across an old stone bridge. Below them, white swans glided gracefully across the River Avon. People were splashing around the river in small boats or picnicking on its grassy banks. Not far upstream, a modern red-brick building dominated the landscape.

"Yon's the Royal Shakespeare Theatre," said McDuff. He was quick to point out several other places of interest on their way to the Shakespeare Hotel, the famous sixteenth-century building where

Honey's parents had arranged for them to stay. They were all excited by the thought of actually sleeping in such an old building.

By mutual agreement, the travelers, after entering the handsome black-and-white, half-timbered construction, headed first for the hotel dining room. They ordered their dinner and were sitting by the bay window, waiting for it to arrive, when Trixie and Honey excused themselves to go wash up.

"Let's go upstairs and look around," urged Trixie once they were heading back to the dining room. "It would be such fun!"

"Shouldn't we get back to the table?" Honey asked. "What if our food arrives—"

"I just want to take a peek at the bedrooms," said Trixie, grabbing Honey's hand. "Mart told me they were named after Shakespeare's plays. You know— like the dining room is named *As You Like It.*"

Honey reluctantly agreed, and the two girls ran upstairs to explore the narrow, hushed, dimly lighted corridors.

"Look, here's *Much Ado About Nothing*," said Trixie with a noisy giggle. "Sounds just like me!"

"Ssshh, people in these rooms might be resting," Honey said. "Anyway, there's the room I want—*A Midsummer Night's Dream.* I'll bet it's darling inside."

Something about the combination of play titles and hotel rooms was enormously appealing to Trixie's funny bone. "Oh, Honey," she cried, "after all the rotten things I've been thinking, I need to have a good laugh!"

"Okay, okay, but just do it more quietly," pleaded Honey. "Oh, how sweet! Here's a room called *Romeo and Juliet*."

"You can have that one! I think these two over here are a scream—*The Tempest* and *All's Well That Ends Well*. Wait till I tell Mart!" Trixie fell to chuckling again, and by the time she reached *The Taming of the Shrew* and *Love's Labour's Lost*, she was almost doubled over with laughter. "Oh, I can't stand it," she shrieked. "Imagine a bedroom called *Comedy of Errors!*"

"Ssshhh," Honey whispered, but it was too late.

A plump chambermaid came bustling down the hall. "The porter says ye're to come down now," she said, her voice quavering with indignation.

The two girls reached their table just in time to hear the proprietor telling the others that, owing to an unfortunate miscalculation, no accommodations were available that night. No reference was made to the girls' behavior, but Trixie was immediately convinced that she alone was responsible for this embarrassing turn of events. If only she had kept her mouth shut and acted properly!

"The natives of Stratford take their Shakespeare pretty seriously," she overheard a tourist at the next table saying.

Miss Trask overheard it, too, and after the proprietor had gone, she turned to Trixie. "We could hear you clear down here in the dining room," she said, her lips set in a thin line. "I can't think how you could be so rude." She turned back to her meal and left Trixie squirming.

"Just her youthful spirits," McDuff said kindly. He then insisted on leaving right away to see what other accommodations he could arrange for them that night.

Dinner was roast duckling with orange sauce, the specialty of the house, but Trixie felt too awful to eat much. The rest of the group were remarkably quiet as well, and the delicious meal was not enjoyed as it should have been.

"You know, Trixie," Miss Trask said, to break the silence after dinner, "you might consider that your behavior in a foreign country could lead its people to dislike all Americans. I know you've been feeling that the English are unfriendly, Trixie, but what about *you?* Have you thought about your actions from their point of view?"

"I—I guess not," Trixie said miserably. Honey squeezed her hand under the table, but that didn't help much.

Since it was late in the evening and the town was jammed with summer tourists, the only rooms McDuff was able to find were in two bed-and-breakfast houses next door to each other. After they got settled, he brushed off Miss Trask's concern about his dinner.

"I'll just get a bite in a pub," he assured her. "Perhaps ye would like to come along for a glimpse of the night life in Stratford?"

The boys agreed enthusiastically, but all Trixie wanted to do was crawl into bed and hide her burning face. Honey, who was sharing her room, insisted on staying with her. Miss Trask hesitated, obviously torn between remaining with the girls and going out with the others.

"Please don't worry about us, Miss Trask," Trixie said earnestly. "We'll be okay."

"Just be *good*," sighed Miss Trask.

"One place ye don't want to miss is the Black Swan, otherwise known as the Dirty Duck," McDuff said as he escorted Miss Trask and the boys out the door. "That's where the Shakespearean actors hang out after the show. . . ."

"I've been thinking," Trixie told Honey, after they got into their pajamas and turned out the light, "about what Miss Trask said about looking at things from other people's points of view. Well, I could start with her and McDuff—I mean, Mr. McDuff. I've been worrying about what if she really fell in love with him and went off to Scotland, or Canada, or wherever."

"Me, too," Honey admitted. "I like Mr. McDuff a lot, but Miss Trask is, well, like my own family. I'd miss her terribly if she moved away."

What Honey didn't say out loud, but what Trixie knew, was that Miss Trask was almost *more* important to Honey, in certain ways, than her own family. Her parents were often away on business, and before Miss Trask had come, Honey had been left in the care of a perfectly horrible governess. Miss Trask was the best of friends to all the Bob-Whites, but especially to Honey.

"But maybe—maybe we are just thinking too much about ourselves," Trixie said. "You know, about how much fun we have when she goes along on our trips, and how she's always there for you when your parents are away."

"And how much help she is to my parents, too," Honey agreed, "managing the estate."

"And even when she's disappointed in me, like tonight," Trixie said, "I just love her. I don't want her to get married and go away. But if *she* wants to—I mean, if it would make her happy, like she seems to be with Mr. McDuff around—well—you see what I mean?"

"Yes." In the darkness, Honey's voice sounded very serious. "Yes, Trix, I see what you mean."

Trixie's resolution to start thinking from other people's points of view was even stronger when she woke up the following morning. Over another delicious English breakfast, the Bob-Whites planned their sight-seeing activities for their first day in Stratford.

"I *have* to see Shakespeare's house," said Mart. "What about you, Trixie?"

"You go ahead," Trixie said. "I have other plans."

"Other plans?" her brother hooted. "Like getting us evicted from another hotel in Stratford?"

Miss Trask shook her head at him. "What did you have in mind, Trixie?" she asked kindly.

"Well, I'm not exactly sure. I just don't want to be a typical Yankee tourist today," Trixie said. "I want to—oh, just walk around." Trixie couldn't explain what she meant. It would sound too corny. She wanted to meet some real live English people and get to be friends with them. Also, she wanted to keep her eyes peeled for clues about the Hart family and Honey's necklace. Often, she could spot things on her own better than she could when she was with a group. And all the worrying about McDuff had been distracting her from the real purpose of their trip—to follow the trail to Honey's English ancestors. She was determined not to fail at that.

"Want me to come along, Trix?" Jim asked.

That was a real temptation, and knowing Jim wasn't mad at her about the previous night made her feel good, too. "Thanks a lot," she said, "but if you came along, all I'd do is talk to *you* all day."

"Well, you're certainly not going to wander around all by yourself," Miss Trask said briskly.

Eventually it was settled that Trixie and Honey would do a little exploring on their own while

McDuff took Miss Trask and the boys to see some of the chief tourist attractions.

"We'll save Ann Hathaway's cottage," McDuff promised. "You girls won't want to miss the place where Shakespeare's wife lived before her marriage."

"I like small towns like this, where you can walk everywhere you want to go," Honey said as the girls set off along Waterside Street, on the banks of the Avon.

They passed the Royal Shakespeare Theatre, and she commented, "Mr. McDuff knows how to get tickets even in the tourist season. Miss Trask says we'll try to go tomorrow, when *Macbeth* is playing."

Trixie knit her brows in an evil leer. " 'Double, double, toil and trouble,' " she chanted nasally, doing her best to imitate Shakespeare's three witches. " 'Fire burn and cauldron—'gleeps!'"

Carried away by her dramatic fervor, Trixie had nearly crashed into two elderly English ladies. At least, she was pretty sure they were English. *Wouldn't you know*, she scolded herself. *Just when I'm reciting Shakespeare through my nose! They probably think I'm making fun of him, like those people did last night.*

But apparently they didn't. Both the ladies smiled, and their nice brown eyes were twinkling. Trixie held her breath. This was her chance to get to know the English point of view!

"We were wondering," she said, "uh—we were

105

wondering—" Trixie's mind went blank. What a time to be tongue-tied!

Honey came to the rescue. "Our friends have gone to see the sights," she explained. "Trixie and I were just looking around." Both girls introduced themselves and smiled their friendliest smiles.

"Have you been in the museum?" the short, stout lady asked.

Yes, Trixie decided, they were English. She could tell from the way they said *been*—as in *string bean.*

The tall one pointed her umbrella up the steps of the building they were standing in front of, right next to the Theatre. "My sister means the Royal Shakespeare Theatre Picture Gallery and Museum," she explained. "With your interest in Shakespeare's plays, you shouldn't miss it. You have an excellent voice, my dear!" she told Trixie.

Trixie turned bright crimson.

"Sister is a speech and drama teacher," the stout woman said.

"And most of my pupils are afraid to open their mouths," the tall one chuckled.

The two women couldn't have been friendlier. Before Honey and Trixie realized what was happening, they had accompanied the girls into the gallery, where there were portraits of Shakespeare and the characters in his plays, paintings of scenes from his works, and costumes and jewelry worn by famous Shakespearean actors and actresses.

The Misses Elizabeth and Mary Tweedie, as they introduced themselves, beamed delightedly as the girls exclaimed over the treasures. Natives of Stratford obviously believed that anything to do with the Bard belonged to them.

"It was so nice meeting you," Honey said warmly as they came out of the gallery.

"Oh, yes!" Trixie blurted. "We were dying to meet some real English people and not just do the regular touristy things."

"Now I see why you Americans think we English are reserved," teased Miss Elizabeth, her brown eyes twinkling. She was the speech teacher. "I don't suppose you would care to have luncheon with us?"

"Oh, do," Miss Mary urged. She was the stout sister and very talkative. "We belong to the Hall's Croft Club, you know. They do delicious luncheons. If you're going to be in town for any length of time, you can join the club for just a few shillings. In any case, you'll be wanting to see Hall's Croft. It was the home of Shakespeare's daughter Susanna and her husband, Dr. Hall. It's a delightful home, furnished with antique—"

"You'll turn these nice American girls into sightseers yet," Miss Elizabeth interrupted, chuckling. "Why don't we just start with luncheon? I'm sure they must be hungry."

At the mention of food, Trixie was immediately famished. Fortunately, Hall's Croft was only two blocks away from the museum and gallery.

Miss Elizabeth recommended the roast leg of lamb, with mint sauce and new peas, and the two girls were happy to follow her advice.

"English food is wonderful," Trixie said between mouthfuls, and Honey agreed. For dessert, they chose fresh raspberries, which started Trixie off on Crabapple Farm. The Tweedies seemed fascinated by everything she said.

"And where are you staying while you're in Stratford?" Miss Mary asked.

"Funny you should ask," Trixie said sheepishly. "Temporarily, we're split up in two different bed-and-breakfast places. We were going to stay at the Shakespeare Hotel, but, er, we got thrown out."

"Oh, Trixie," Honey protested. "Miss Trask said it wasn't that at all. They just found out they didn't have room."

Trixie told the two women the whole story, and by the time she finished, they were red in the face from laughing so hard.

Miss Elizabeth dabbed at her eyes with a handkerchief. "I wonder," she said, "if you would be interested in staying at a country place. A friend of ours is opening up his home to tourists. It's not far out— less than a mile from the center of town. It's hard to find rooms at the height of the season, but Andrew Hart has just renovated his home, and I believe it's opening this week. It's an awfully nice place."

"Did you say Hart?" Trixie's spoon clattered to the floor, and Honey's eyes were enormous. "H-a-r-t?"

"Why, yes, dear," Miss Elizabeth said. "They are calling it Hartfield House."

"Gleeps, Honey," Trixie said. "We're on the trail!"

A Hostile Host · 9

Just wait till we tell them the news!" Trixie's blue eyes danced with glee as she plunked herself down on the bench where she and Honey had arranged to meet Miss Trask and the boys.

"The Belden-Wheeler Detective Agency is on the job," Honey crowed, plopping down beside her.

"Right—while they're off sight-seeing." Trixie wrinkled her freckled nose.

"I would like to see some of the sights," Honey admitted. "It was fun in London, but I think I'm going to like it even better here. The Tweedies were so nice that I hated to say good-bye to them."

"We only have till Sunday," Trixie reminded her.

"Your mother is coming to pick us up Sunday morning, and it's Tuesday already."

"I can't believe it," Honey said. "As somebody or other once said, time sure flies when you're having fun!"

"Well, it's kind of slowing down right now," Trixie said impatiently. "I'm dying to tell Miss Trask and the boys about Hartfield House. Where *are* they?"

Trixie and Honey looked around the grassy park on the riverbank. They knew they had the right bench, in front of the theater.

"I think I see them coming—way down the river," Honey said. "There—see the tall one with red hair and—yes, there's Mart, too. But where's Miss Trask?"

"Elementary, my dear Honey," Trixie said sadly. "She's with McDuff."

"I thought you liked him better now." Honey looked troubled.

"Well—maybe I do, and maybe I don't. But do *you* want Miss Trask to go off with him forever and ever?"

"No, that would be awful," Honey said in a small voice.

"Sorry we're late," Jim called. "You should have gone with us. We saw—"

"Shakespeare's bed!" Mart exploded.

"Well, I bet it's not as comfy as the beds we're going to sleep in tonight," Trixie said excitedly. "What would you say to the Hartfield House?"

"Hartfield House?" Jim's green eyes were puzzled. "Where's that?"

"The *Hart*field," Honey stressed.

"What gives?" asked Mart. "I didn't think Valentine's Day was for another couple of months."

Trixie and Honey looked at each other and grinned.

"We're talking," said Trixie, "about the *H-a-r-t*-field House, recently opened for tourists by Andrew *H-a-r-t*. And if you'll tell us where Miss Trask is, we'd better go make reservations for tonight."

"Terrific!" Jim applauded. "Bird dog Trixie is on the scent!"

"Not to mention hound dog Honey," Mart said. "But I still—"

"Well, where is she?" Trixie interrupted. "Where's Miss Trask?"

"I think she and Mr. McDuff went on a boat ride," Jim said. "They said they'd meet us at The Cobweb for tea."

"The Cobweb." Mart smacked his lips. "That's number one in my gourmet guidebook to a gastronomical gratification."

"Well, we just ate," began Trixie, exchanging glances with Honey. "But you know me. . . ."

"Let's go!" agreed Honey.

On the way, the girls brought Jim and Mart up-to-date on their new friends, the Tweedies, and the boys filled them in on their tour through Shakespeare's many haunts.

"We saw some sights, too," Honey said, and she went on to tell about the museum and gallery. "Brian would love Hall's Croft," she concluded. "After lunch, we went through Dr. Hall's dispensary, where they have old medical instruments and a journal of his cases and how he cured them."

"We're still seeing sights," Jim pointed out. They were approaching a row of black-and-white Elizabethan buildings on Sheep Street, and one of them had a sign that read THE COBWEB.

"Right—a sight for sore stomachs," Mart quipped.

The moment they went through the door, they were surrounded by mouth-watering cakes and confections of every kind, which were for sale behind a counter on the lower floor. Upstairs, the Bob-Whites slid in behind a gleaming oak table near an old brick fireplace. As they started reading the menus, there was no sign of Miss Trask or McDuff.

"Let's just go ahead and order," Mart said.

"The Cobweb could catch fire, and Mart would still say, 'Let's go ahead and order,' " Trixie teased.

"I thought 'tea' meant tea and maybe some cookies," Honey said, looking over all the selections on the menu.

"Biscuits," Jim corrected her. "In England, cookies are called biscuits."

"Then what are biscuits called?" Trixie asked.

"I think they're called something like scones," Jim said doubtfully.

113

Before they had that matter settled, a comfortably plump waitress appeared to take their orders. "Wot'll y' 'ave, duck?" she asked Honey.

"No, thanks. I think I'll have Welsh rarebit," Honey said, "and a pot of tea."

Her three friends burst into giggles, much to Honey's bewilderment. Her manners, on occasions such as this, were as elegant as her mother's. What on earth was so funny?

"Oh, my sides," Mart moaned. "Help! I'm going to split!"

"She was *calling* you duck," Jim managed to explain, "not asking you if you wanted any."

"And 'ow about you, luv," the waitress said to Trixie.

Trixie stifled a chortle. She didn't want to provoke another international incident. "I'll have a selection of gateaux," she decided, "please."

Jim ordered the same, and Mart said, "I'll have tongue salad, and the finger sandwiches, and a sausage roll, and some pastries, and—"

"Mart," Trixie protested, "this is tea, not Thanksgiving! Ease off!"

It was their waitress's turn to giggle, and she was still chuckling when she returned with their food.

" 'Ere y' are, ducks," she said. "Injoy!"

Halfway through the meal, McDuff and Miss Trask appeared. They sat down at a table nearby, and Miss Trask leaned over to speak to the Bob-Whites.

"I'm sorry to keep you waiting," she said. "You see, we were rowing—and somehow I lost my oar. I've never done anything so clumsy in my life. It just floated away, and Gordie and I had quite a time getting it back."

Gordie! Trixie and Honey looked at each other in horror, and Mart's sandy eyebrows shot up half an inch. They had barely recovered from that shock. when they received an even greater one.

"What will you have, Marge?" McDuff was saying—to Miss Trask!

"Jeepers," Trixie whispered. "Nobody ever—"

"Sshh," Jim whispered back.

"Is that her name?" Mart asked under his breath.

"It's Margery," Honey said. "I've seen it on the letters she gets from her sister." She forced a pleasant expression onto her face as Miss Trask looked over at them and smiled.

Trixie swallowed hard. *Now, they're adults,* she reminded herself sternly, *which means that they can call each other whatever they please. And anyway, that's not so important now that we're back on the track of Honey's ancestors.* She couldn't wait to get on with the case.

When the four friends had eaten the last crumbs of their delicious afternoon tea, they moved over to Miss Trask's table, and Honey and Trixie filled her in on the Tweedies and Hartfield House.

"The Tweedies said they'd be glad to recommend

115

us," Trixie said, "and that there's sure to be a vacancy because they're just opening up this week, and besides, Honey is probably related to them, because her great-great-aunt Priscilla who left her the necklace was a Hart, and when Mrs. Wheeler comes on Sunday, she'll be so thrilled to find us living in her own ancestral mansion, probably, and—"

"Whoa, there, Trixie!" Jim laughed. "You're extrapolating quite a bit."

"He means," Mart explained, "that you're extending your knowledge of a known area into conjectural knowledge of an unknown area."

"He means," Miss Trask said, "that you're exaggerating again, Trixie." The familiar twinkle in her nice blue eyes made the Bob-Whites feel that maybe she hadn't changed all that much, after all. "By all means," Miss Trask added, "let's go see Hartfield House. It sounds lovely, and I don't like being separated, the way we are in our present lodgings. That is, of course"—she turned to McDuff—"if you agree?"

"Your word is my command, luv," he said heartily, beaming at her.

The word *luv* didn't mean anything special in England, Trixie knew. Perfect strangers were always saying *luv* or *duck* or *dear*. What bothered Trixie was that when McDuff said it to Miss Trask, she blushed! One minute, Trixie thought, Miss Trask was her old self, and the next minute she was a whole different person. *The Bob-Whites will have to have an emergency meeting and do something about this*, she decided silently.

Hartfield House was about a mile out of town on Welcombe Road.

"Jeepers, imagine your very own relatives living this close to Shakespeare," Trixie said to Honey. "They probably bumped into him in the grocery store, or wherever they shopped in those days!"

"It all adds up," Honey said thoughtfully. "If the Shakespeares lived so close to the Harts, it wouldn't be that surprising for Shakespeare's sister to marry a Hart. So that must mean that the tradition that we're descended from Shakespeare is really true!"

Unfortunately for that theory, Hartfield House didn't look anywhere near as old as the half-timbered Elizabethan buildings the Bob-Whites had seen in Stratford-on-Avon. It was a beautiful mansion, however.

"Well, the original Hart house could have burned down, and then they built another one," Trixie guessed as McDuff guided the Maroon Saloon into the crescent driveway.

The two-and-a-half-story pink-brick mansion was surrounded by bright-colored flower gardens. Emerald green ivy climbed the walls to a gabled roof that had dormer windows and more chimneys than they could see to count. The front entrance was protected by a grass-paned vestibule, which sparkled in the glow of the late afternoon sunshine.

The Bob-Whites held their breath as they waited inside the enclosure. Were they going to get to stay in this beautiful mansion? And was it really owned by a member of Honey's own family?

McDuff rapped on the door with a gleaming brass knocker that was in the shape of a deer.

"Deer . . . Hart!" Mart exclaimed softly.

"Dear heart?" Trixie repeated. "Who on earth are you talking to, Mart Belden?"

"A male deer," her brother explained patiently, "is a hart. Ergo, the family emblem."

It seemed like a long time before a brown-haired woman in a plain black dress opened the door a crack. "Yes?" she said coldly.

"We heard you have rooms to let," Miss Trask said, then hesitated. "But perhaps this isn't the right place. . . ."

"Come in," the woman said grudgingly, and she opened one of the lace-curtained double doors.

The Bob-Whites filed in, followed by Miss Trask and McDuff. The woman disappeared through a hallway in the rear, leaving them standing in the reception hall.

"Wow!" Trixie marveled. "I've never seen so many colors!"

"It's beautiful!" Honey's eyes were shining. "Just wait till Mother sees it. Everything blends so well— the different shades and tones. . . ."

"It's what Mrs. Wheeler would call a decorator's dream," Miss Trask agreed.

"I know what Trixie means about color," Jim said. He looked from the deep-purple-carpeted reception hall, with its antique furniture slipcovered in blending mauves and lavenders, to a pink and gray parlor at one end and a crimson-walled dining room at the other. "I never would have expected an English home to be brighter than we'd have in America!"

"It rains a lot here," McDuff explained with a chuckle. "A bit of color warms it up."

"Surprisingly enough, the stereotyped ideas we have about people of other nations are more often false than true," Mart said earnestly. "You know, like I thought that the English would have terrible food. That was certainly an elephantine prevarication!"

"Big lie," Jim translated helpfully.

"I have a hunch that more surprises are on the way," Trixie said under her breath.

A strikingly handsome dark-haired man in full dress had emerged from the hallway at the rear. "Yes?" he said, repeating the monosyllabic greeting of the woman in the black dress. Under arched black eyebrows, his dark eyes were sardonic.

To Trixie, he looked like a mad scientist from a monster movie, but she was so eager to talk to him that she couldn't keep quiet another minute. *And besides*, she thought bravely, *the way to make friends is to be friendly*, *like we were with the Tweedie*

119

sisters. It worked fine with them.

"Are you Mr. Hart?" she asked brightly.

"Andrew Hart," he said.

"Andrew! That's the name of my favorite uncle," Trixie rushed on. "And we're just dying to stay in your hotel because we think Honey—this is Honey Wheeler—well, her ancestors—on her mother's side— were named Hart! So she might even be related to you, and—"

"That will do, Trixie," Miss Trask interrupted quietly. "Mr. Hart, we do hope you have accommodations for us for the rest of this week. We understand that you have only just opened your beautiful home for guests."

"You have been misinformed," Mr. Hart said icily. "We have not yet finished with the necessary renovations." He walked to the front door and held it open. Before the group knew what was happening, they were standing outside in the gravel driveway.

"Gleeps." Trixie tried to swallow the lump in her throat. "It looks like I did it again."

"It wasn't your fault," Honey said soothingly. "You were just being friendly, like you were with the Tweedies. Most people appreciate your friendliness. Don't worry about it, Trixie."

"Methinks our host has something against us," Mart agreed.

"I think it was something else," Miss Trask remarked thoughtfully. "Something that has absolutely nothing to do with us, personally."

Well, I *think Andrew Hart is a bit of a meanie*, Trixie thought privately. *And I kind of hope that Honey's not related to him!*

Anne · 10

McDuff HEADED straight for the Maroon Saloon, and the Bob-Whites followed him. Miss Trask lingered behind to admire the red, yellow, and orange mums and marigolds bordering the crescent drive in front of Hartfield House. The Bob-Whites were about to climb into the backseat, when the vestibule door opened, and a girl came running out.

She was about Trixie's height but very slender, and she seemed a little older. She had dark brown hair cut in a smooth and shiny pageboy style, and she was wearing a blue and white tennis outfit. Her eyes were a very dark blue.

"Hullo," the girl said forthrightly, holding out her

hand to Miss Trask. "I'm Anne Hart. My father says you are looking for lodgings."

The Bob-Whites gathered around her. She looked as though she might have been crying, but perhaps, thought Trixie, it was just the English strawberry-and-cream complexion that made her cheeks seem so pink.

"We understand you're not ready to open yet," Miss Trask said pleasantly.

"But Miss Tweedie—" Trixie began.

"Yes, we know the Tweedie sisters," said Anne. "Actually, they rang us up to ask if we could accommodate a party of six." Anne flushed even pinker and went on breathlessly. "We *are* still in the process of renovation, which my father felt might inconvenience you. But we do have a few rooms we could make available."

"Are you sure?" Miss Trask asked. "We wouldn't want to inconvenience *you*."

Anne smiled. "If you can put up with us, we'd be glad to put you up," she said in her straightforward way. "Would you like to see the rooms? I'm afraid they wouldn't all be adjoining. We have three dormer rooms ready on the second story, and then there's a twin bedroom opening off the rose garden."

"Oh, Miss Trask, could Honey and I have that one?" cried Trixie. "It sounds fantastic!"

"What do you think?" Miss Trask asked McDuff, who had joined them in the driveway. "Should we go ahead and look at the rooms?"

"Anything ye say, Marge," he told her.

Anne showed them the rooms herself. Andrew Hart and the gloomy woman in black were nowhere to be seen.

The bedrooms turned out to be as colorful as the entrance area. It was hard to believe that their forbidding host had authorized this imaginative interior decoration. The dormer rooms were done in different color schemes—a blue and gray one for Miss Trask, green and gold for McDuff, and a medley of reds for the boys.

"When Mother sees how gorgeous this place is, she'll probably go home and redo our entire house," said Honey with a little sigh. Manor House could be hard to live in when Mrs. Wheeler was on one of her redecorating sprees.

The loveliest room of all was the Rose Room. It had its own separate entrance from the large garden behind the mansion—a garden with pebbled paths and vine-covered bowers, a maze of hedges, and roses, roses, roses! The room was mostly white, with white furniture and white-canopied beds, but the wallpaper was covered with pink roses, and there were bowls full of pink blossoms fresh-picked from the garden outside.

"You're our first guests," Anne said, "although we do have a number of bookings for next week."

"Then you can practice on us," Trixie laughed,

and Anne smiled back at her. She had a lovely smile.

"We'll run back to town now and get our things," Miss Trask said.

"Would you like dinner tonight?" Anne asked. "I'm afraid my father won't be here. He's off to the theater."

"Oh, no," Miss Trask assured her. "We'll eat in Stratford tonight. And we're hoping to attend the play tomorrow night."

"Jolly good," said Anne. "We serve dinner at six for the theatergoers. As you probably know, the price of the room includes dinner and breakfast."

And the prices Anne quoted, agreed the group once they were back in the Maroon Saloon, were so reasonable that they would have been foolish to stay anywhere else.

Overjoyed, Trixie slouched down in the backseat. *Not only are we staying in what is probably the prettiest house in the whole country*, she thought, suppressing a howl of glee, *but we're also in a perfect position to really get cracking on our case. Now, if we could just do something about McDuff. . . .*

Immediately after breakfast the following morning, Trixie called an emergency meeting of the Bob-Whites.

"We're all chiefs and no Indians at this meeting," commented Jim. He and Trixie were copresidents of the club; Honey was vice-president, and Mart was secretary-treasurer. "Too bad Brian, Di, and Dan can't be here. Anyway, what's this all about, Trix? I understand we're here to save Miss Trask from a fate worse than death."

"This is no time for jokes," said Trixie, her blue eyes flashing. "I wish the others could be here, too, but we can tell them everything when we get home. We have to act fast! Did you hear McDuff at breakfast this morning? Can you *believe* all those icky things he says to Miss Trask? I told you, I just don't trust that man!"

"You were worried he was going to steal our money," Mart said lightly, "and now you're worried he's going to steal our chaperon."

"It's not funny," Trixie insisted. "Maybe it's not so bad for you, Mart, but what about Honey and Jim? And what about Mr. and Mrs. Wheeler? What are they all going to do without Miss Trask? How can we sit back and let this happen? After all they've done for us!"

"Are you saying she's going to elope with Mr. McDuff to Scotland at the end of the week?" Jim asked. "That's pretty fast work, even for a con man— if in fact that's what he is. And besides, Miss Trask isn't the type to get conned that easily."

"She's only having a little fun for a change," Mart added. "And who are we to stop her? What do you think, Honey?"

"I don't know what to think." Honey was almost in

tears. "She isn't acting a bit like herself, and I don't want her going off to Scotland or wherever. But I don't want to be selfish, either. I—I guess we ought to be happy for her."

"Honey, you're being so romantic," Trixie sighed. "We don't know a thing about the man. For example, what about that huge roll of bills he asked Anne to put in the safe for him last night? I think there's something—"

"Strange about him," the others chorused.

"He may not be a professional con man, like I thought at first," Trixie went on stubbornly. "He did bring our money back, and he did save Honey's life, but I can't help it. I simply don't *like* him. All that stuff he says to Miss Trask sounds so phony."

There was a short silence.

"I have to admit I don't quite trust this whirlwind courtship, either," Jim said finally, and Trixie could have hugged him.

"Well, what are we going to do about it?" she demanded.

"The main thing we have to consider is Miss Trask's feelings," Jim said slowly. "We don't want her getting hurt—by us or by Mr. McDuff. So we don't want to do anything rash."

"Right," said Mart. "If we butt in and she doesn't want us to, we could lose her even sooner than you think, Trixie."

"So it looks like we'll have to take a wait-and-see

attitude," Honey said thoughtfully, "and not do anything till we have more to go on."

The boys agreed and turned to Trixie.

"I suppose you're right," said Trixie. Her friends were always so cautious. But then, she herself was often too hasty.

Whatever McDuff's intentions were toward Miss Trask, the Bob-Whites became aware that they couldn't have found a better guide. By the end of a day of sight-seeing around the nearby countryside, with McDuff at the wheel, even Trixie had to admit that they'd had a marvelous time. And they had gained a little knowledge about their case, besides.

That night, the four Bob-Whites talked over the day's discoveries as they waited for dinner to be served in the Crimson Room at Hartfield House. They were also waiting for Miss Trask and McDuff, who had decided to get dressed for the theater before their dinner.

Each of the young people had seen sights that day that had had particular appeal to his or her interests and ambitions.

"As far as the Belden-Wheeler Detective Agency is concerned," Trixie said near the end of their long discussion, "the most important thing was getting to see Shakespeare's father's house and his mother's house. It's wonderful to be able to get such a clear picture of how the Shakespeares lived. And I just can't get over how all those four-hundred-year-old houses are still in such good shape!"

"His mother's house was what got me," Mart said. "Mary Arden's farm. With a dairy and all those old milk pails and things they made cheese and butter with, and a cider mill—"

"And the stable!" Jim added enthusiastically. He was crazy about horses.

"And all those old plows and sowing and harvesting gadgets," Mart went on. "I could have stayed there a week."

"I thought Mary Arden's house was beautiful," Honey agreed. "I just love these old Elizabethan kitchens, with those huge stone fireplaces and big brass pots."

"No dishwasher, though," sniffed Trixie.

"That's right," Mart said, poker-faced. "No one had got around to inventing Trixie Beldens by the sixteenth century!"

"I wonder if almost-twin brothers had been invented then," said Trixie sweetly. "Anyway, what am I complaining about? I'm getting out of all my chores at home for a whole week!"

"Me, too," said Mart. "Except for the chore of keeping my little sister in line!"

Before Trixie could think of a retort, Honey said, "I wonder what's keeping Miss Trask and Mr. McDuff. If we don't get started with dinner soon, we won't have time to get properly dressed for the theater."

"What are you wearing, Honey?" Trixie asked her friend anxiously.

"Well, I notice that Anne's father has been going to the theater every night, and he's been wearing a tux, so I suppose that means we should wear our very best."

Mart clapped his hand to his forehead. "Good heavens!" he cried. "We've forgotten our tuxes, haven't we, James?"

Jim nodded ruefully. "That's right, Martin. I guess we'll just have to wear our jeans, won't we?"

"You *can't* wear *jeans*—" Honey began, and then she noticed the twinkle in Jim's green eyes. "You guys are too much," she snorted.

Jim whistled, an appreciative gleam in his eyes. He wasn't looking at Honey, however.

McDuff and Miss Trask were entering the dining room—and Miss Trask was wearing an evening gown! It was a soft shade of pink, with a high neck, long sleeves, and a skirt that swished elegantly around her silver sandals.

Trixie couldn't remember ever seeing Miss Trask in anything other than one of her trim, tailored suits. "Jeepers, Miss Trask," she blurted without realizing how tactless she sounded, "I didn't know you wore dresses like that!"

"You look perfectly beautiful," Honey assured her.

"Even more pulchritudinous than usual," agreed Mart brightly.

"Thank you, everyone," Miss Trask said crisply. "Now, if people will kindly take their eyes off me, I believe there's a dinner to be eaten."

The dinner, which turned out to be delicious, was served by a jolly, apple-cheeked English lad in his late teens. Besides the woman in black, who they'd found out was Mrs. Hopkins, the housekeeper, he and the cook seemed to be the only servants at Hartfield House.

Midway through her fresh strawberry shortcake, Trixie realized that Miss Trask hadn't been eating very much throughout the meal. She had mentioned at one point that she was too excited about seeing *Macbeth* at the Royal Shakespeare Theatre, but that confused Trixie. It wasn't like Miss Trask to be, well, *excited.*

Another thing that confused Trixie was how strangely quiet McDuff was being. In fact, now that she thought about it, he always talked a great deal on their sight-seeing trips, but he hardly ever seemed to say a word inside Hartfield House . . . particularly when Mr. Hart or Anne were around.

After dinner, the boys rushed upstairs to put on their seldom-worn suits. As the girls were getting into their dresses, Trixie tried to discuss the new mystery with Honey.

"Why d'you think McDuff's so quiet all of a sudden?" she asked. "If ever an icky compliment was called for, what with Miss Trask looking so fabulous at dinner and all, you'd think now would be the time."

Honey shrugged. "Maybe he was struck dumb," she giggled.

The moment they were on their way to the theater in the Maroon Saloon, however, McDuff was off again with his extravagant praise. "Och, but ye're the pink of perfection this evening," he told Miss Trask.

"Nonsense, Gordie," she answered. "Everyone in the car looks perfect tonight."

" 'The lady doth protest too much, methinks,' " Mart quoted under his breath.

"I think you mean that something is rotten in the state of Scotland," Trixie muttered back.

"That's Denmark," Jim said softly. "And anyway, both of you have the wrong plays. We're going to see *Macbeth* tonight, remember?"

The Royal Shakespeare Theatre, from the old stone bridge, was a blaze of golden lights shining across the dark river. Tourists in evening dress were milling around the entrance as the Bob-Whites made their way through the crowd. McDuff bought programs, and then they all settled down in their seats.

To Trixie's delight, they were sitting in the front row. "It's the closest thing to actually being on stage," she said.

Honey was reading all about *Macbeth* in the program. Suddenly she whispered, "Trix, look!" She leaned over and put her finger under the name of one of the actors in the cast of characters.

" 'Third murderer,' " Trixie read from the program. " 'Gregory Hart.' "

Gregory · 11

DURING INTERMISSION, McDuff urged the Bob-Whites to go have an ice. "It's a tradition in the British theater," he told them.

Trixie wasn't sure whether it was tradition or the chance to be alone with their chaperon that McDuff was more interested in, but the young people were happy to follow the crowd to a balcony overlooking the Avon. The golden lights of the theater were reflected enchantingly in the river.

An ice turned out to be lime sherbet in a cardboard cone.

"After all that blood and gore in the play," Mart said appreciatively, "this really hits the spot. And I don't mean the 'damned spot,' either."

"*Macbeth* must be the bloodiest play Shakespeare ever wrote," said Honey with a slight shudder.

"Right," Trixie chortled. "For all the special effects, they probably go through a case of catsup bottles a night!"

Just then, Anne and Mr. Hart walked up to the Bob-Whites. Trixie wanted to dive into the Avon. Here she was, surrounded by sophisticated theatergoers in an elegant theater, and she was snickering about catsup! Andrew Hart looked more than ready to turn on his heels and stride away, but Anne had her hand tucked firmly into the crook of his elbow.

"Yes, *Macbeth* is a hard play to produce," the English girl said easily. She looked lovely in her long, midnight blue dress, and her father was very handsome in his tuxedo. Trixie, on the other hand, was unaccustomed to dressing up and was feeling distinctly uncomfortable.

"Well, I think it's great!" Jim said. "I never dreamed I'd be seeing the Royal Shakespeare Company playing *Macbeth* in Stratford-on-Avon. You and Anne are fortunate to live so close by, Mr. Hart."

Trixie's face was red-hot, but to prevent herself from seeming an utter idiot, she felt she ought to contribute something besides catsup to the conversation. "We noticed a Gregory Hart in the cast," she said politely. "Are you related?"

"Yes, he's my brother," Anne said. "He's—"

135

"If you will pardon us," Mr. Hart said stiffly, "we should return to our seats now."

"I was wondering why he comes every night," Trixie said once the Harts were out of earshot. "His son's in the play. So Gregory Hart is a real live actor, and he may turn out to be Honey's cousin or something!"

"Probably something twice removed," Honey said with a rueful smile.

The real live actor turned out to be a really lively boy, as the Bob-Whites found out when they met Gregory Hart the following morning after breakfast. He was about Jim's age and looked a great deal like Andrew Hart except for his friendly grin.

"I'm frightfully sorry you didn't get to come backstage after the play last night," Gregory told them. "Perhaps another time."

"Backstage!" Trixie said. "Jeepers, that would be neat. I think it's perfectly marvelous that you're an actor in the Royal Shakespeare Company."

"It's only a bit part," Gregory said modestly. "I just hang around till they can't get rid of me any other way."

"He's been doing that for years," Anne said with an affectionate smile. "He learns all the parts—the small ones, you know—in case he should be needed. And now they count on him."

"What's on the agenda for today?" Gregory asked.

"Have you been to Shottery yet?"

"Anne Hathaway's cottage," Anne explained.

"We're not just here to see the sights," Trixie told Gregory. "You see—"

"But we do want to see Anne Hathaway's cottage," Honey interrupted eagerly. "We can't miss that, Trixie."

"My sister, the famous detective," Mart drawled, "can't be bothered with mere sight-seeing. *She's* here to solve a mystery."

"A mystery!" Anne clapped her hands. "How smashing—can we help?"

It was decided that Anne and Gregory would go along on the pleasant walk across the fields to Shottery, and on the way, Trixie and Honey would fill them in on their current case. Unfortunately, Miss Trask and McDuff joined the party. Trixie was almost certain that McDuff knew nothing about Honey's necklace, and she wanted to keep it that way. However, that proved to be no problem. As usual, the big Scotsman was keeping Miss Trask entirely to himself, and they lagged far behind the young people.

"My mother was very much interested in genealogy," Anne said after Honey had told them about her great-great-aunt Priscilla Hart. "I'm sure we could find some of her charts."

"Wouldn't it be smashing if Priscilla turned out to be on one of the branches of our family tree?"

137

Gregory said with an admiring glance at Honey's golden hair.

Uh-oh, thought Trixie. *Brian had better watch out.* Back in Sleepyside, Honey and Brian had always had a special interest in each other. *Of course, Honey's so attractive that people take a special interest in her wherever we go*, Trixie thought fondly.

When Trixie described the necklace and Honey related what the appraiser had said about it, Gregory and Anne both looked thoughtful.

"Elizabethan, you say, but not real jewels?" Gregory frowned. "But if the necklace is a copy, couldn't it have been made much later?"

"I don't know," Honey confessed. "That's just what the appraiser told my mother."

"You'd think they'd have some way of dating the materials," Jim said, "or maybe the workmanship."

"The way you describe it, it sounds like something I've seen somewhere." Anne knit her delicately arched brown eyebrows. "But I can't seem to remember where."

"Oh, really?" asked Trixie, pouncing on a promising-sounding lead. "Well, the necklace is in your father's safe at your house. If we show it to you tonight, do you think you'll remember?"

"Possibly," Anne said.

"But we wouldn't want to bother your father," said Honey. "I'm afraid we've been such an inconvenience to him already."

"Oh, Father," Anne said a bit crossly. "I'm frightfully sorry he's been such a bore. He simply hates having to take in guests."

"He refused to do it for the longest time," Gregory said. "But it came down to putting up with the tourists, or selling the family home."

"My mother finally persuaded him." Anne's face saddened. "That was before she died. She did enjoy doing over the rooms."

"They're so beautiful," Honey said softly.

"After she died, Father wanted to go back on his word," Gregory said, "but we couldn't let him. The rates kept going up, you know—the taxes."

"No wonder your father is so—so sad," Honey said.

Trixie felt awful. Why couldn't she ever understand why people acted the way they did? Anne shouldn't have had to explain it.

No one said anything for a while. It was a beautiful sunny day, with a few cloud-puffs in the sky. Soon the footpath came to an end. There, across the road, was the famous thatch-roofed cottage of Anne Hathaway, surrounded by shrubs, bright flowers, and herbs of every kind.

"Shakespeare got a lot of his poetry right from this garden," observed Mart.

"Please—no more quotations," Trixie said. "I can't believe how big this house is! I thought it was just a little cottage."

"English cottages aren't so small," Miss Trask said.

She and McDuff had caught up with them, and they all joined the queue of tourists that was filing through the old two-story farmhouse where Will Shakespeare had come to woo Anne Hathaway. The wooden bench on which they were supposed to have sat still stood in the kitchen by the large open hearth. The rough, flagstone floors and raftered ceilings were picturesque, and all the rooms, upstairs and down, were furnished with authentic furniture. McDuff and the Harts took turns pointing out items of interest.

"The Tweedie sisters live up the road," Anne told the Bob-Whites after they had finished the tour. "Would you like to drop in on them? They've just bought their own place, and they're as pleased as punch about it."

Trixie was delighted at the chance to show off her and Honey's special English friends.

"You'll love them, Miss Trask," Honey said.

"They're just about your age," Trixie added.

Miss Trask didn't seem to appreciate that remark. "Since I plan to do some research at Oxford University tomorrow, this afternoon is my last chance to do some shopping," she said tartly. "You children go visit your friends. We'll see you at dinner."

And off she went—with McDuff!

"Dinglebuckles," Trixie said, stamping her foot. "There they go again."

Gregory burst out laughing. "Jolly good word," he said. "Where'd you find it?"

140

"Oh, I don't know," Trixie said. "It just seems appropriate right now."

"You don't like the man much, do you, Trixie?" Anne asked.

"How did you guess?" Mart put in.

"To tell you the truth, we've been wondering where you met up with him," Anne went on.

"In London," Trixie said. "I thought he was in one of those tourist rackets at first—you know, a con man. But it turned out he wasn't."

Gregory and Anne listened attentively to the Bob-Whites' jumbled report of how McDuff had come to be their guide.

"Is he registered with the London Tourist Board?" Gregory asked.

"I don't know," Honey admitted. "He just arrived from Canada, but he said he had been a guide before."

"Ordinarily, you shouldn't hire a guide that isn't registered," Anne said. "But of course, if he saved your life—"

"Oh, he did," Honey said earnestly. "I was practically under that huge bus, and he pulled me out."

"I can't explain *why* I don't like him," Trixie said to Anne. "It's just that he seems so—so phony!"

Anne and Gregory looked at each other, as if they didn't know whether they should say something or not.

"I think we should tell them," Anne said.

Just then, Miss Mary Tweedie came bursting out of the side door of a large thatched cottage that looked just like Anne Hathaway's.

"You've come to see our new home," she cried, her round face rosy with excitement. "Isn't that lovely? Elizabeth will be so pleased."

"Where *is* your house?" Trixie looked up and down the road, but she couldn't see anything that looked like a house. Honey and the boys looked puzzled, too, much to the Harts' amusement.

"The Tweedies have bought a home in Hathaway Hamlet," Anne explained, pointing to the big thatched cottage. "I expect in America you would call it an apartment."

"Just one up, one down, and a wee garden," Miss Mary said proudly.

The Bob-Whites were more puzzled than ever.

Miss Elizabeth was waiting to greet them inside the wooden gate. "Do come in," she said heartily.

Their "apartment" consisted of two main rooms— one upstairs and one downstairs, as Miss Mary had said. A small staircase next to the fireplace led to the bedroom, and there was also a modern kitchen and bath, with the "wee garden" at the back door. The white plaster walls and dark-beamed ceilings were distinctly Elizabethan.

"It looks just like Anne Hathaway's cottage, only it's cut up into apartments!" Honey exclaimed. "And there's a whole row of them."

142

"It's even older than the Hathaways'," Miss Elizabeth said.

"Now that we own property," her sister chimed in, "we are called City Burgesses and can vote in the Council."

"And pay the rates," Miss Elizabeth added wryly.

"So Hathaway Hamlet is a thatched condominium," Mart chuckled.

It was the Tweedies' turn to look puzzled.

"Usually, apartments are rented in the United States," Mart explained. "But sometimes people buy into a building, and they call it a condominium."

"A thatched condominium," Miss Elizabeth repeated, and the sisters laughed delightedly.

After serving their visitors a delicious tea, the Tweedies escorted them back to the wooden gate, and the Bob-Whites set out across the fields again with Anne and Gregory.

Trixie turned around for one last good-bye wave to the Tweedies, and then she whirled back to the Harts. "Please," she said, "tell me what you were going to say before—about McDuff."

The Harts looked at each other again, and Anne nodded. "Tell them, Gregory," she said. "They really ought to know."

"Well—mind you, I'm not saying he's not a proper chap," the English boy said reluctantly. "But. . . ."

"Gregory has studied acting, and he's been around very good actors all of his life," Anne said, "and he

143

thinks—go on, Gregory, tell them!"

"It's just that he's no Scotsman," Gregory said.

"What do you mean?" gasped Trixie.

"That accent's as phony as the wig I wore in the play last night," Gregory said simply.

To Market, To Market · 12

BEFORE DINNER that evening, the Bob-Whites held a brief emergency meeting and decided against telling Miss Trask what Gregory had told them.

"Maybe his accent sounds different because he's lived all those years in Canada," Honey said.

"Well, if we notice anything else suspicious, I think we should tell her everything we know," insisted Trixie.

"Let's keep our eyes and ears open," said Jim. "But in the meantime, he's going to Scotland in a few days, anyway. We can tell her after he's gone."

After dinner, the Bob-Whites met with Gregory and Anne, who got the necklace out of the safe for them and came into the Rose Room to examine it.

"Ah, now I know what it reminds me of," Anne said, then hesitated. "But perhaps I shouldn't mention it, in case I'm wrong."

"Oh, tell us," begged Trixie and Honey.

"Well, are you going to be visiting Warwick Castle?" Anne asked.

"The famous medieval fortress with all the priceless artwork inside?" asked Mart. "Yes, McDuff said something about taking us there the day after tomorrow."

"What I'm thinking of is in the Great Hall there," Anne said. "I'll try to arrange it so I can go there with you, but if I can't, I'm sure you'll be able to spot what I'm talking about." She looked at her watch and opened a folder she had brought in with her. "It's getting late, but I did want to show you these genealogy charts that our mother made."

By the time the Bob-Whites finished poring over the charts, they were too sleepy to do more than say good night. They were still yawning over breakfast in the Crimson Room the following morning, although an announcement from Miss Trask soon jolted them awake. They had been planning on spending the day in the Bodleian Library at nearby Oxford University, but Miss Trask had apparently thought better of it.

"Gordie and I will head over to Oxford by ourselves," she said. "The Bodleian Library is an excellent old library, and it does have some genealogical material on the Harts, as well as an exhibit of Elizabethan jewelry. But we've decided that it would be a shame for you youngsters to spend a whole day in research when there are so many interesting things to do here in Stratford."

"Yes, ye simply must visit the Stratford Market," said McDuff with an emphatic roll of his *r*'s. "Stratford's always been mainly a market town, ye know, and it's quite an attraction for the tourists."

"To market, to market!" Mart said good-naturedly.

To buy a fake Scot, Trixie thought to herself with a toss of her sandy curls.

After McDuff described the market further, Honey said politely, "It sounds like what we would call a farmer's market back home. It'll be fun—we have lots of shopping for souvenirs to do, anyway."

The Bob-Whites decided to head for the market in the afternoon, because Anne and Gregory had offered to entertain them at Hartfield House that morning. The two Harts were too busy running the house to spend more than a few hours at a time having fun. Andrew Hart appeared to avoid any menial labor, and there didn't seem to be enough servants for all the work. Gregory's apprenticeship at the theater kept him busy, also. Both Anne and Gregory looked wistful whenever any of the Bob-Whites mentioned anything about their club or their friends back home.

First the Bob-Whites helped the Harts clean up the stables, and then Gregory asked Jim to go riding.

147

There were only three horses in the large stables, and Andrew Hart had already galloped off on a handsome black stallion. Anne let Jim use her mare—a prancing roan with a star on her forehead.

"Let's play tennis," Anne said to the others. "We can play some doubles if you like."

"Anne is a tournament player," Gregory told them before he cantered off with Jim. "She's too bashful to mention it herself, but she got to the semifinals at Junior Wimbledon this year."

"Gleeps," groaned Trixie. "She'd better not pick me for a partner. I'm the pits as far as tennis is concerned. I never seem to find the time to practice."

"Tennis takes patience," Mart said, "a virtue foreign to Trixie's tempestuous nature."

The Bob-Whites hadn't brought their tennis gear, but Anne had enough rackets to go around, and they took off their shoes and played barefoot. The Harts had a grass court that felt cool and soft to their feet.

"You're not so terrible," Anne told Trixie once they started playing. "You just need more confidence, that's all. You're a jolly good partner!"

Trixie and Anne proceeded to trounce Mart and Honey for several games until Jim and Gregory came back from their ride.

"You played great, Trix," Honey said that afternoon as the Bob-Whites set off for the market.

"Anne's a wonderful partner," Trixie said. "Not just because she's so good, but she made me feel like I was playing super, so I played better."

Everybody laughed at Trixie's garbled explanation, but they knew what she meant.

"Feeling confident helps in any sport," Honey agreed.

"I wouldn't have missed that grass court for anything," Trixie said. "I'm just as glad we didn't go to that library."

"Me, too," Jim said. "I think I'm in love—with a horse!"

"And we really do have to get some presents today," Honey added. "We don't have much time left."

"True," Trixie said. "But what we *really* have to do is solve our mystery—in two days."

"We do have some leads," her partner reminded her. "Those charts Anne's mother made, and whatever it is Anne's going to show us at the castle. And then there's the information Miss Trask finds out today in Oxford."

"If any," Trixie scoffed. "I doubt if she gets any work done with that Transylvanian or whatever hanging around all the time. I just can't help wondering—"

"What he *is*," Mart interrupted understandingly. "Why would he pretend to be Scottish if he isn't?"

"And what's he buttering up Miss Trask for?" Trixie added, surprised to have Mart on her side for a change.

"What makes you so sure he doesn't *mean* what he

149

says to Miss Trask?'' Honey asked, looking troubled. ''Older people do fall in love sometimes, you know, and she's a wonderful person.''

''Honey could be right,'' Jim said. ''When you think about it, what's the man done to us? Merely saved Honey's life, showed us around to all the best places, and given Miss Trask a good time—which she sure deserves.''

''He's going to break her heart,'' Trixie insisted.

'' 'A pair of star-cross'd lovers,' '' Mart quoted with a sigh.

''Isn't that from *Romeo and Juliet?*'' asked Trixie. ''They're not exactly McDuff and Miss Trask!''

Honey was looking more and more upset, and Jim tactfully changed the subject. ''It must be hard on Gregory and Anne to run Hartfield House,'' he said. ''All that work, and not enough money for servants, and their father so bitter about the whole thing. Anne may have to give up her tennis, Gregory told me.''

''But she's really good,'' said Trixie.

''He didn't say,'' Jim went on, ''but I suspect he may have to give up his acting career, too, if they can't make a go of it.''

''A lot of English families with big old homes have that problem,'' Mart said. ''The taxes—rates, I mean —are so high that they either have to sell their homes or take in tourists.''

''The inflation makes it hard to maintain a large house, too,'' Jim added.

150

"I wonder what would happen if my father lost his money and had to rent out rooms in Manor House." Honey's big hazel eyes filled with sympathy.

"We'd manage," Jim said. "I'm sure Dad could take it, but. . . ."

"I know," Honey sighed. "It would kill Mother."

"Well, anyhow, we cleaned up our rooms this morning," Trixie said. "So maybe Anne and Gregory can meet us at the Cobweb for tea, like they were hoping."

"Yes, they simply must try the duck," Mart said with a teasing look at Honey.

Like every place in Stratford, the market square was within walking distance, even from the Harts' country mansion. After passing the Post Office, the Bob-Whites found Wood Street, which led to the American Fountain. This statue, which Anne had directed them to, stood at the center of the open space where rows of booths had been set up. Not only farm products, but also tourist souvenirs and other colorful miscellanea were displayed.

"Good chance to get some more pictures," said Mart, putting a roll of self-developing film into his camera.

"Jeepers, this is almost as crowded as Piccadilly Circus," Trixie observed as they joined the throngs of shoppers.

"Anne said we might want to check out the regular shops in town, too," Honey said. "I want to look in that china store she told us about. I just have to get some of those cute cups and bowls with bunnies on them for Bobby and the Lynch twins, and some china flower baskets for Mother—"

"Oh, my gosh!" Trixie cried. "Look at that!"

Jim, Mart, and Honey craned their necks to see what she was pointing at.

"There—over there! Oh, quick, Mart, give me your camera!" Trixie waved wildly at the statue in the center of the market square.

"You want a picture of the American Fountain?" Mart handed his sister the camera with an indulgent grin. "I happen to know it was presented to Stratford-on-Avon in the year of Queen Victoria's jubilee. A jubilee, in case you're wondering, is the fiftieth year of the reign of an English monarch. That was in the nineteenth century, in the year—"

Without waiting for him to finish, Trixie yanked the strap of the camera over her sandy curls. She didn't hear what year, but she did remember to look in the viewfinder and aim carefully before clicking the shutter. "Oh, please, let me do it right," she muttered. "Just this once."

"Here," Mart chuckled. "Don't waste too much film, Trixie. Just tell me what you want. I'll take it."

"What's up, Trix?" Jim asked more seriously.

"I saw him!" Trixie insisted. "Right by the statue. And this time you'll *have* to believe me."

"Saw whom?" Honey was used to Trixie's some-

152

times indefinite way of talking and could often read her mind, but this time she was completely baffled.

"You'll see," Trixie promised. "Here, Mart, take out the picture."

As Mart slid the developed photo out of the camera, Trixie could hardly wait to snatch it from him. Teasingly, he held it up, just out of her reach, and looked at it himself.

"Not bad," he said. "Not bad at all, Trix. Hey, guys, this is the best picture Trixie has ever taken!"

"I didn't jiggle it," she agreed. "And I know I didn't cut off his head—come on, Mart, please give it to me!"

Mart handed her the snapshot.

She took a quick look and groaned. "It was Gray Cap!" Trixie fought back tears of frustration. "He must have slipped behind the statue just after I focused. I held my breath for a second to make sure I wouldn't blur it—that must have been when he got away. Oh, *dinglebuckles.*"

Jim, Honey, and Mart were silent. Trixie almost wished they'd tease her about her overactive imagination, but they were being strangely tactful. Oh, she knew she'd have to have proof before they'd ever believe she'd seen that London pickpocket way out here in the country. And she had taken a perfect picture, too, not the least bit jiggled—only it was of a statue!

"Better luck next time," Mart said after a while. He

153

actually sounded almost sympathetic.

For Trixie, the shopping trip was spoiled. She bought some things for the folks back home, but she hardly noticed what. She was still keeping her eyes peeled for that dirty gray golf cap.

The Bob-Whites were back at Hartfield House by six. Gregory had shown up for tea at The Cobweb, but Anne hadn't been able to make it. She met them in the garden, where she was picking some flowers for the dining room.

"Mariellen, the cook, had a spot of trouble with the joint," she explained. "I had to lend a hand."

"A joint," Gregory added, "is a roast. Well, I'm off to the theater now. See you all later."

Trixie and Honey walked along the rose-lined path to their room, to freshen up before dinner. "Honest, Honey, I did see him," insisted Trixie. "I'd know him anywhere."

"I suppose they do have pickpockets in the country," Honey admitted. "In places like Stratford-on-Avon, with all these sightseers. But I don't see how it could be the same one, Trix. We're ninety miles from London! One piece of jewelry wouldn't be worth following us all this way."

"Unless it was a *crown* jewel," Trixie said.

"But it isn't. It's only glass, the appraiser said." Honey stood on tiptoe to pick a pink rose from the trellis that arched the Rose Room door.

"I wonder if Miss Trask and McDuff will be back

in time for dinner," Trixie said as she pushed open their door. "Hey—that's funny. It isn't locked."

"Oh, Trixie!" Honey's voice quavered as they looked around their room, once beautiful but now in a shambles. Their suitcases were in the middle of the beds, wide open. Clothes were strewn around the flowered carpet. The bedcovers were even ripped off the beds. Their things were spilling out of the bureau drawers.

The girls stared at each other with tears in their eyes.

"How *awful*," Trixie whispered.

Honey was rummaging in a drawer. When she turned to face Trixie, her face was drained of color.

"My necklace," she squeaked. "We were so tired last night, and I meant to ask Anne to put it back in the safe this morning. But oh, Trixie, I forgot, and now it's gone!"

Family Tree · 13

EVERYBODY FORGETS sometimes," Trixie said as comfortingly as she could.

"But n-not s-such an *important* thing." Honey couldn't stop crying as they rushed up the stairs to Mart and Jim's room.

Trixie pounded on the door, but nobody answered. Had they gone down to dinner already? Just as Trixie was about to give up, Jim opened the door. He had just finished washing his hair. It was dripping wet, and he had a towel around his shoulders. Mart, they saw, still had his head in the washbowl.

"Come see our room!" Trixie cried. "It's all messed up, and Honey's necklace is gone."

"Have you called the police?" Jim asked quickly. "When did it happen?"

"We don't know. Sometime when we were gone," Trixie said. "Anybody could have got in through the rose garden, because the door was unlocked, and—"

"I know I locked the door," Honey said positively. "I remember that."

"It had to be Gray Cap," Trixie said. "I told you I saw him in the market square—"

"Come on," Mart interrupted. "Let's go! Wait—no, wait a minute. Where's my wallet?" Mart's head was still plastered with curly white lather, but Trixie had never seen her brother so excited. Mart, the unflappable!

"It's right there on the bureau," Jim said.

"Yeah—well, look!" Mart riffled through the wallet and came up with a snapshot. He held it out to Trixie. "Is that the guy?" he asked her.

Trixie couldn't believe her eyes. There he was, that creepy little gray man, half hidden in the crowd around the American Fountain.

"Mart," she squealed. "That's him!"

"He," Mart corrected mechanically. "I was planning to surprise you all at dinner, but you'd better see it now. I saw him a few minutes after you did, Trix, and got a pretty good shot. Should we show it to the police?"

"You're darn tootin'!" Trixie's blue eyes sparkled. "Oh, Mart, you're *wonderful*. Come on!"

Trixie led the charge down the stairs to the kitchen.

"Anne! Anne!" Trixie yelled in the little hallway that led to the kitchen.

The swinging door opened, but it was Andrew, not Anne, Hart who stood there, glaring at them. "Yes?" he said curtly.

"Oh, Mr. Hart, we've been robbed," Trixie blurted, while Jim was saying, "We'd like to call the police, sir," and Mart was delivering a lengthy explanation of how he took his picture. Honey was too upset to say a word.

"Indeed?" Andrew Hart's black eyes snapped, and his nostrils were white with anger. "Anne?" he called, turning his back on them. When she came hurrying out, he disappeared into the kitchen, leaving the Bob-Whites to tell her all over again about the robbery.

"Oh, dear, I'm most frightfully sorry. We must ring up the constable immediately," she said. "Poor Father! He must have been terribly upset. We've never been burglarized, you know."

Before the local police had time to arrive, the Maroon Saloon drove up in the gravel crescent, and McDuff handed Miss Trask out with a flourish. The Bob-Whites and Anne were all waiting at the door.

"She looks like she had a wonderful time," Honey murmured to Trixie. "She's positively glowing!"

"All the worse for her when McDuff takes off for Scotland," Trixie muttered, "if that's where he's really going. I'll believe *that* when I see it."

"Well, even if he isn't a real Scotsman, he hasn't done us any harm," Honey said. "He certainly couldn't have taken my necklace—he was in Oxford all day."

"True," Trixie admitted reluctantly. "I guess he couldn't. But anyhow, we know who the thief was."

The constable arrived while McDuff and Miss Trask were dressing for dinner. The young fellow in blue went over the Rose Room thoroughly without coming up with a single clue, but he promised to do more investigating.

At dinner, the girls went over the whole story again.

"It could have been a pickpocket who ransacked the Rose Room, *but*," Miss Trask said crisply, "he didn't get Honey's necklace!"

"Didn't get it?" Anne, Honey, and Trixie said in one breath.

"I asked Gregory to put it in the safe before I left this morning," Miss Trask explained. "Didn't he tell you?"

"He's been at the theater," Anne said weakly. "He doesn't know anything about all this."

"Oh, Miss Trask!" Honey said gratefully. "I've been feeling so awful."

"I knew you took it out last night, and I just thought I'd better check to be sure it got put back," their chaperon said.

"I forgot," Honey confessed miserably.

"Well, no harm done." Miss Trask's blue eyes were sympathetic. "It's easy to forget things when you're excited, even important things. Actually, I've been wondering about something myself. You say the door of your room was open when you got back? I got Gregory to open it for me with the master key, but I can't remember for the life of me if I latched it when I left."

The Bob-Whites stared at each other in amazement. Their Miss Trask—the embodiment of efficiency—*forgetting* something?

After dinner, Trixie and Honey straightened up the Rose Room. "I bet that constable never catches up with Gray Cap," Trixie said.

"Do you think he'll try again?" Honey asked anxiously. "Gray Cap, I mean?"

"Sure to," Trixie replied. "But that's when we'll catch him."

The Bob-Whites were traveling light, and it didn't take the girls long to put things back in the drawers and hang clothes up in the closet.

"I can hardly wait to go to the castle tomorrow," Honey said. "I've never seen a real castle, have you?"

"Nope. But what I can't wait to see is whatever-it-was Anne was talking about—you know, in the Great Hall."

"What if her father won't let her go with us?" Honey worried.

160

"He's got to," Trixie said confidently. "Now 'come along,' as the English say. Let's go hear what Miss Trask found out at Oxford today."

At dinner there had been so much talk about the pickpocket and the ransacked room that Miss Trask hadn't had a chance to tell the Bob-Whites about her research on the Hart family. They had agreed to meet in the drawing room an hour after dinner, and Miss Trask had urged Anne and her father to join them. Gregory, of course, was still at the theater. He had a small part in *A Midsummer Night's Dream* and had got some good seats for his houseguests for the Saturday night performance.

There was a fire crackling on the hearth of the pearl-gray-carpeted drawing room, and the boys were sitting rather gingerly on two beautiful antique chairs. Miss Trask and McDuff sat on a sofa, and Anne was poking the logs. Mr. Hart, as Trixie had expected, was not there.

"I think we'll have an interesting report for Mrs. Wheeler," Miss Trask began, riffling through a sheaf of papers covered with genealogical ladders. "I couldn't find much on the necklace, but starting with Will Shakespeare's sister's marriage to William Hart, I have just about traced the Harts to a Thomas Hart who came from London to Hanover County, Virginia, in 1690. His great-grandson, Thomas Hart of Kentucky, married a Miss Gray of North Carolina. Their third son, Benjamin, was the one who married

161

Nancy Morgan, the Revolutionary heroine. In my preliminary study in the United States, I had already traced your aunt Priscilla's line back to the same Thomas Hart. So we have a pretty convincing family tree."

"So Honey really is descended from Shakespeare's sister Joan?" Mart asked.

"Almost certainly," Miss Trask said. "There is a 'missing generation' in English history—during the time of Oliver Cromwell in the 1650's—when many records were destroyed, and genealogists trying to trace their families all the way back to Anglo-Saxon times often run into this snag."

"I'm sure we're some sort of cousins," Anne said, smiling at Honey. "Mother's charts show a connection with the Thomas Hart who went to the States!"

"But what about the necklace?" Trixie wailed. "Here we are, supposed to be detectives, and it's Friday night and we have to go home on Sunday, and all we've done is almost lose Honey's inheritance!"

"It's not too late for you to solve your mystery," Anne said. "Wait till you see what I've got to show you in the castle tomorrow."

"Terribly sorry to intrude."

Everyone looked up to see Andrew Hart standing in the arched entrance to the drawing room. His voice was as formal as his customary evening attire.

"Father!" Anne jumped up and ran to his side. "Do sit down. Miss Trask has found out the most frightful lot about the Hart family at Oxford today.''

"Indeed." Their host raised his heavy black eyebrows. "I take it you are planning a trip to Warwick Castle in the morning?" he said to Miss Trask.

"Yes, Mr. Hart, that was our plan," she replied crisply.

Trixie grinned. Good old Miss Trask!

"Breakfast will be served at eight then," Mr. Hart said. "If that is satisfactory. Come along, Anne. I must talk to you immediately. There's a great deal to be done before Monday."

"Can she come to the castle with us?" Trixie blurted out. "Oh, please, Mr. Hart. We could all help you get ready for the people who are coming next week."

"That will not be necessary," he said. "And in any case, I'm sure you will find people to give you a guided tour at the castle. Like all of us," he added bitterly, "they cater to tourists."

Warwick Castle • 14

SO IMPATIENT was Trixie to explore Warwick Castle that the Bob-Whites found themselves, along with Miss Trask and McDuff, standing outside the gray stone fortress several minutes before it actually opened. Anne's father had not given permission for Anne to come with them, but Gregory had promised to drive her over as soon as they were finished with their chores.

"Gordie's been telling me how important women have been in the history of this castle," Miss Trask said as they lined up with the other tourists in front of the gate. "For example, in the tenth century, it was Alfred the Great's daughter Ethelflada who built the very first parts of the castle."

"Probably to defend herself from jokes about her name," chuckled Mart. "Ethelflada!"

"Another powerful lady in the history of Warwick was Felice," Miss Trask went on. "Her husband went off on a pilgrimage, and for many years, during the Crusades, Felice held the fortress."

"The lady who ruled the castle in the thirteenth century was named Margery," said McDuff, twinkling at Miss Trask.

"Not to mention a much more recent Marjorie, who served in the British Expeditionary Forces in the First World War," Miss Trask informed him with a smile. "She was a Mayor of Warwick, too."

"Hey, look—a guard is opening the gate," said Trixie.

The Bob-Whites bought their tickets and hurried through the archway in the massive stone walls that surrounded the castle. A long, winding drive was cut through the stone, and huge evergreens towered above them on both sides, blotting out the sunlight. McDuff and Miss Trask wandered off toward the formal gardens, with the understanding that the young folks could take the guided tour.

"We'll catch up with you," Miss Trask promised. "I want to get some ideas for the garden at Manor House."

"And ye must see the peacocks," McDuff added, taking her arm.

165

Jim whistled. "What an impregnable fortress! These walls look ten feet thick, and it looks like this driveway is the only way to get in."

"That wall over there rises almost a hundred fifty feet above the river," Mart reported after consulting his guidebook.

"Does it say anything in there about Guy's Tower?" asked Trixie. "I've heard it has a secret staircase we could explore."

"It's not open to the public," Mart said after a moment's search.

"We can see the dungeons, though," said Jim. "Sounds like something Trixie would go for."

"Let's go to the Great Hall first," Honey said. "Isn't that where Anne said we'd find a clue about my necklace? Oh, I do hope she gets here soon!"

"I wouldn't count on it," said Trixie gloomily. "The police haven't come up with anything yet on the Rose Room break-in, and Mr. Hart seems angrier than ever. You know—I suppose you guys will think that I'm really getting carried away, but do you think there's any chance that he's the one who broke into our room?"

"You certainly are getting carried away," Jim scolded. "Why would he want to get such bad publicity for Hartfield House?"

"And besides, he's not like that," added Honey. "Trixie, you just don't trust anyone anymore! I know you still think Mr. McDuff is a phony. I'll have to admit I don't think he sounds all that sincere, either, but I'm prejudiced. I don't want to lose Miss Trask. And I can never stop being grateful to him for saving my life."

"I've been thinking about that," Trixie said darkly. "And you know what I think? That he could have pushed you off that curb himself, just so he could pretend to save you!"

"Trixie Belden!" Honey gasped. "What a horrible thing to say! Why would anyone do a thing like that?"

"To get in with us," said Trixie. "That could be why he borrowed my money and then paid it back—so he could gain our confidence and get to be our guide."

"But why would—" Honey broke off as other tourists clustered around and the tour began.

The tour guide was a tall Englishwoman with a booming voice. After listening to her for a minute, Trixie leaned toward Honey and the boys.

"Do you think we could just go around by ourselves?" she whispered. "She sounds kind of boring."

"But these are terribly famous painters," said Honey, waving toward the wall. "Just these few pictures must be worth thousands."

"And the castle is full of them," Mart said. "Rubens, Van Dyck, Perugino, Sir Joshua Reynolds, even Rembrandt, not to mention all sorts of other art treasures. I'm with Trixie, though. We can get along just with the guidebook, can't we, gang?"

The others agreed and hung back to let the rest of the group go on ahead. They then passed through several rooms, marveling at the exquisite treasures and listening to Mart relate interesting facts from the guidebook.

"This is all fascinating, but when do we get to the Great Hall?" As usual, Trixie was forging ahead. "Is this it?"

Mart joined her in the doorway of an enormous room with its furnishings cordoned off by tasseled ropes. "Yep, this is it," he said.

The massive stone walls of the Great Hall were paneled in oak, and heavy timbers arched across the ceiling. The floor was a huge checkerboard of red and white marble. Along the wall opposite the doorway was a large collection of weapons and shining silver armor, but two of the suits of armor were only an arm's length from the Bob-Whites, within the ropes.

"I hope those tin suits are empty," Trixie giggled.

"Oh, look at the little one," Honey cried, pointing to a child-sized coat of mail.

"It's just about big enough for Bobby," Trixie said.

"It belonged to the son of the Earl of Leicester," Mart informed them. "He was nicknamed 'The Noble Imp.'"

"I bet he was a cute little boy," Honey said.

"Somebody didn't think so." Mart grinned ghoulishly. "He died—probably by poison—before he was even a youthful eight years old."

"Please, spare us the details," Honey implored.

"Hey—come over here," Jim called. He was standing by one of the windows in the castle wall, outside the roped-off area, looking down at the river far below.

"It's beautiful!" Honey exclaimed.

The rough water of the falls frothed and sparkled in the sunshine. Even Trixie was spellbound for a minute—until she remembered their quest.

"Did anybody see anything in the Great Hall that reminds you of the necklace?" she asked. "Oh, I wish Anne would get here!"

"Let's look hard," Honey suggested.

"It couldn't be anything connected with the collection of armor, could it?" Jim asked.

"Let's see." Mart consulted his booklet. "They have the supposed sword of the redoubtable Guy of Warwick, and the Saddle and Cloth in the Tudor colors of green and silver that belonged to Queen Elizabeth. Also, the helmet of a crusader, a knight in fifteenth-century German armor on a horse in English armor, the helmet of Oliver Cromwell, the leg piece and gauntlet of the Black Prince—"

"It couldn't be anything like that," Trixie said impatiently. "What else is there?"

"Well—there's that huge metal caldron called Guy's Porridge Pot. It was used to cook up meals for all the troops back in the fourteenth century—"

Trixie shook her head gloomily.

"The marriage chest of Isaac Walton? One of those wood carvings?"

"No, no. Even if there was any jewelry, we couldn't get close enough to see it." Trixie wrinkled her forehead, thinking hard.

"Something in one of the tapestries, or a painting?" Honey asked. "Maybe it was a *picture* of a necklace that reminded Anne of mine?"

"Honey, you're a genius!" Trixie spun her around with a big hug. "Look!"

She pointed excitedly at a portrait of Queen Elizabeth the First on the wall directly opposite them, hanging above the collection of armor and carved chests. She wore her crown and coronation robes of brocade and ermine, and carried a scepter in her left hand and the jeweled globe called the Queen's Orb in her right.

"So? She's wearing the crown jewels," Mart said. "We saw them already in the Tower of London."

"Strain your eyes and look around her neck," Trixie squealed.

A heavy gold necklace, glittering with huge jewels, hung in a wide circle around the royal shoulders.

"It looks *exactly* like mine," Honey said incredulously. "Oh, Trix, it can't be!"

"I wish we had some binoculars," Mart grumbled.

"This *must* be what Anne was talking about," Trixie said. "She knows this castle inside and out."

"Watch out, Trix," Jim said suddenly.

Trying to get a closer look, Trixie was pressing up against the rope that cordoned off the furnished area of the Great Hall. Before she knew what was happening, the old rope broke, and Trixie crashed into the nearest knight in armor. With a loud *clank*, they both landed on the checkered marble floor!

Her face flaming, Trixie scrambled up with as much dignity as she could muster. The others asked her if she was hurt, and she shook her head.

"Trixie strikes another blow for international relations," Mart sighed.

The stout, red-faced castle guard who appeared didn't see anything funny about Trixie's little spill. Trixie expected a stern lecture, but the guard merely glowered at her and began setting up the armor.

A crowd of curious tourists had gathered, accompanied by the tall Englishwoman who was giving them the tour and who was properly indignant at Trixie for leaving her group.

Her freckled face was still pink, but Trixie forgot all embarrassment at the sight of Anne Hart rushing down the hall.

"Oh, Anne, if only you'd got here two minutes sooner," Trixie groaned. "I was trying to get a closer peek at that portrait of the queen over there. That *was* what you wanted us to see, wasn't it?"

"Righto. Don't you think they're a lot similar?" Anne's dark blue eyes sparkled with excitement, but she kept her voice low. They were surrounded by tourists, and the Englishwoman was shepherding them along to the next room.

"They couldn't be exactly the same," Honey murmured, "because Queen Elizabeth would never have worn fake jewels."

"Your necklace could be a copy," Trixie said. "But what would they have made a copy *for*? If we could figure that out—"

They had reached the next roped-off chamber, and Trixie was drowned out by the powerful voice of their guide. "This is the Red Drawing Room," the Englishwoman said. "It is paneled in red and gold, and. . . ."

Trixie wasn't listening. "Imagine having a necklace just like Queen Elizabeth's," she whispered, squeezing Honey's hand.

The tourists passed from the Red Drawing Room to an even larger one, paneled in cedar. It was magnificently carpeted and filled with priceless antiques.

"Gleeps!" Trixie said. "It has *five* chandeliers!" She was bug-eyed. The Wheelers and Di Lynch's family both were extremely wealthy, but they couldn't begin to furnish rooms like these. "I'd sure hate to have to live here, though," she said. "You'd never know when you'd go crashing through the ropes!"

"I'd take Crabapple Farm any day," Honey agreed. She smiled at Trixie.

"The beds don't look too comfortable, either," added Trixie when they reached the State Bedrooms.

"Oh, look," Honey cried. "Just look at that adorable doll's furniture—over by the fireplace. That cute little sofa and those armchairs are covered with tapestry just like the big ones."

"Actually, they were all samples of Louis-the-Sixteenth furniture sent from France, to obtain orders for the full-sized furniture," Anne said, "but I've always hoped some little prince or princess got to play with them."

"It's so fascinating to see all these treasures from different periods of history and different countries—all in one place," Honey said.

"And not all jumbled up together in glass cases, the way they are in the museums we visit on field trips at school," Trixie agreed. "It's much more fun to explore a castle. And speaking of exploring, I'm dying to go up in one of those dark towers. I've seen enough furniture!"

The number of sightseers in the castle had increased, and as the Bob-Whites made their way through the passage toward the courtyard, Trixie had a sudden urge to look behind her. That was when she caught sight of an old familiar figure.

Jim was walking beside her, and she clutched his arm. "Jim! Look! There's Gray Cap!"

"Where?" He swung around, but not in time. The figure had disappeared.

"Oh, why am I the only one who ever sees him?" Trixie wailed.

"Are you sure it was Gray Cap?" Jim asked.

"Sure, I'm sure. Hey—everybody!" She waited impatiently for Mart, Honey, and Anne to join them. "I saw the pickpocket back there in the crowd. He must have ducked behind a column."

"Right," Mart said. "I saw him, too."

"You did?" Trixie gasped. "Well, then, come on— let's catch him!"

A large group of tourists had emerged from the shadowy castle halls into the courtyard. For a moment, the Bob-Whites were blinded by the bright sunlight, and then Trixie saw the man again.

"Look! He went into that tower!" She pointed to the tower at the northeast corner of the battlements.

Miss Trask and McDuff came up just then, and Trixie hastily filled them in. "Mart saw him, too," she said excitedly. "He's *still* following us."

"But what can we do about it if he is?" Miss Trask asked practically. "We could never prove it's the same man that took Honey's handbag in the Tower of London. Not that I believe for a minute that that man has followed us all the way from London."

"But Mart took that picture of him," Trixie insisted, "in the Stratford market square. And we're just positive he's the one that ransacked the Rose Room. He's after Honey's necklace!"

"Marge tells me ye two lassies have quite a record

as girl detectives," McDuff said. "But what do ye propose to do with the man if ye catch him?"

"Well, we could confront him," Trixie said. "We could let him know we're onto him. What are we supposed to do—just let him go free?"

"Ye have a point there," McDuff said thoughtfully. "But I thought this necklace ye're referring to is locked up in the safe at Hartfield House."

"It certainly is," Miss Trask assured him. "And there it will remain till Mrs. Wheeler comes to pick us up tomorrow morning."

"However," McDuff continued, "I see no harm in trying to flush this little fox. I promise ye I'll give him a talking-to he won't soon forget. Come along, then. We'll muster our troops."

Jim and Mart had gone on to the foot of the narrow, winding stairs to the tower Trixie had pointed out. The rest of the party joined them.

"Jeepers, Mr. McDuff," Trixie said gratefully, "that's awfully nice of you."

"My pleasure," he said. "Now, how do ye want to go about it?"

"We could bottle him up in the castle," Trixie said eagerly. "He's up in this tower now—he must be, unless there's some other way out. And anyway, he'd have to go down that long driveway to get out of the castle grounds. It's tunneled out of solid rock and too high to climb, and there's the porter at the gate—"

"I'll cover the gate," Mart said.

175

"Perhaps I should do that," McDuff was protesting, but Mart had already taken off, long legs flying.

"*Is* there any other way out?" Trixie asked Anne.

"There is another breach in the walls," Anne said, "but it's always guarded. They'd never let a stranger out there, but in any case, I'll go speak to the guards." Anne's dark pageboy bob bounced on her shoulders as she ran across the courtyard.

"Jim and I will smell the man out," McDuff said grimly. "You ladies stay here. I'll climb the tower, and Jim can reconnoiter, in case the little rat slips out. Those pesky little thieves have a way of slipping right through yer fingers." The big Scotsman disappeared up the dusky stairway.

"Stay here?" Trixie fumed. "Not on your life!" And she was off before Miss Trask could say a word. If McDuff was going up that tower, so was she. "Ladies," indeed!

The stone steps were narrow and so twisted that there wasn't room to set both feet on one stair. The light was dim, and Trixie stumbled. A sharp pain shot through her ankle, but she hardly noticed it.

"Just take 'em one at a time," she muttered to herself.

She thought she heard Miss Trask calling for her to come down, but she decided she wasn't sure about that. Anyway, McDuff was right ahead of her. What could happen? He was twice as big as Gray Cap!

On the way up, she passed several small rooms

with slits in the stone walls, for shooting arrows at attackers. Trixie examined each room to make sure that the little gray man wasn't hiding in any of them. She found nothing until the last room, where there was a painting on the wall. For one awful second, she could have sworn that the eyes in that painting were following her. Trixie set her jaw, looked closer, and decided there was no way anyone could be hiding behind it.

"Brrrr," she shivered. It was cold in the murky stone tower.

After that, the steps grew even narrower, and there were no handrails—only a rope to hang on to.

"I hope this rope's not as old as the one in the Great Hall," she muttered, clutching it tightly.

Finally she caught sight of sunshine through an opening above her. She stopped to catch her breath, and for a moment she thought she heard voices. She raced up to the stone parapet. If McDuff was giving Gray Cap that talking-to, she wanted to get in a few words herself!

But there was nobody in sight on the parapet.

The blue sky was filled with huge white clouds, and the rolling green hills of the Cotswolds stretched out below her. From this corner of the battlements, she couldn't see the river.

Suddenly the big Scotsman appeared from around a bend in the parapet. When he caught sight of Trixie, he looked angry, she thought. But then he smiled.

"Och, lassie!" He shook his grizzled head at her.

"Ye came after all. But as ye can see, there's nobody here."

"I'll just walk around and take a look," Trixie said. She was almost positive she had heard voices up here. And who could it have been but Gray Cap and McDuff? Unless, of course, Gordie McDuff talked to himself, like she did sometimes. . . .

"No, ye will not," McDuff said firmly, and his big hand bit into her arm as he piloted her ahead of him down the narrow stairs. "Just what would a wee lass like you have done if ye had met up with a dangerous criminal instead of with me?" he asked sternly.

Trixie tossed her curls defiantly. Maybe he didn't mean to, but McDuff was hurting her arm.

A Midsummer Night's Dream · 15

DIDN'T YOU HEAR me calling you?" Miss Trask asked as Trixie and McDuff joined the others in the court-yard. "We have to leave now. The castle is closing."

"But we can't leave now," Trixie protested. "We can't let Gray Cap get away again."

"He has to be here somewhere," Honey agreed. "I went and talked to Mart down at the gate. He and the porter both say nobody could have come down that drive without their seeing him."

"The guards I talked to said the same thing," Anne reported. "And that's the only other breach in the walls."

"I looked everywhere that's open to the public,"

Jim said. "I sure would hate to play hide-and-seek in this castle. There are a million hiding places."

A stout, red-faced guard beckoned impatiently from the Clock Tower. "Move along, now," he called.

"I think he's the one that popped up when I fell in the Great Hall," Trixie whispered to Honey.

"I don't know what we would do if we did come across the man," McDuff was telling Miss Trask.

Trixie overheard him and looked indignantly at Jim. "I bet he doesn't even want to catch Gray Cap," she muttered. "It would probably delay him on his trip to Scotland."

"Well, it is a sticky problem, Trix," Jim told her. "We have to leave tomorrow, too, you know. Even if we had enough evidence to make charges, we wouldn't be here for the trial. And as I said, I doubt Andrew Hart will want to advertise what happened to the Rose Room. So perhaps he won't even press charges."

Trixie couldn't believe her ears. Even Jim was ready to give up the search!

She marched up to the stout castle guard. "There's a pickpocket hiding somewhere on your grounds," she informed him. "He followed us all the way from London, where he snatched my friend Honey's purse. But the thing he was looking for wasn't in it, and then we saw him again in the market square yesterday—in Stratford—and last night our room at the Hartfield

House was ransacked, so would you please let us stay and look for him?"

The guard seemed completely befuddled by Trixie's impassioned appeal. "Are you the young lydy as caused the disturbance in the Great Hall this afternoon?" he inquired.

Not seeing what that had to do with anything, Trixie was unsure how to continue.

"Come, Trixie, there really isn't anything further we can do," Miss Trask called.

"Well, then, will *you* look for him?" Trixie asked the guard. "And will you call us up and let us know if you find him?"

"You could ring us up at the Hartfield House in Stratford," Anne said. "And reverse the charges. My father is Andrew Hart."

"I know the gentleman," the man puffed importantly. "And if there's anybody shut up in Warwick Castle, which I doubt, 'e won't get out till the gytes open tomorrow."

"The castle doesn't open till one o'clock on Sundays," Anne said as she and the three Bob-Whites hurried down the drive to the outer gate, followed by McDuff and Miss Trask.

Trixie looked up at the sheer stone walls on either side. No one could possibly climb them. This late in the afternoon, not a single ray of sunshine filtered through the giant treetops above.

Trixie shivered. "I wouldn't like to spend the night

here myself," she told Honey.

"Not even in one of those fancy beds?" Honey laughed.

"Don't *you* want to catch that man?" Trixie asked suspiciously.

"Well, as Mr. McDuff said, what could we do if we did? After all, we're going home tomorrow, and I don't think he'll follow us to Sleepyside! My necklace is safe, and we've solved our mystery."

Not as far as I'm concerned, Trixie thought.

Mart was waiting for them at the outer gate. He came up close to his sister and muttered in her ear, "I told the porter all about Gray Cap. He says they'll look around."

"I'm glad somebody takes me seriously," she told Mart gratefully.

"The porter says there's no way anybody could get out after the gate is locked," Mart went on. "All Gray Cap can do is wait and try to slip out when the crowds come tomorrow. He'll probably figure we stopped looking for him."

"He'll be wrong—we'll be here," Trixie said grimly, her jaw set.

The Bob-Whites stayed to watch the closing of the gate. As the solid, impenetrable wood gate swung shut, the porter waved at them with a conspiratorial grin.

Soon the Maroon Saloon was kicking up the gravel in the crescent drive of Hartfield House. As usual,

McDuff hurried around the car to open the door for Miss Trask.

Trixie and Honey walked through the rose garden to their room. "I sure do hope he doesn't break her heart," Trixie muttered to her best friend. "If he's off to Scotland tomorrow morning, do you think she'll ever hear from him again?"

"When you were up in the tower, Miss Trask told us he plans to come to Sleepyside after he gets back home," Honey said. "He lives in Nova Scotia."

Trixie's arm still hurt where McDuff had grabbed it. In fact, as she noticed when she changed into her prettiest dress, it was turning purple. She decided not to mention it to Honey, though. Not yet.

They had to hurry through another delicious dinner in order to get to the theater by curtain time.

"It seems as if we've been rushing from one place to another ever since we got to England," Honey said. "But isn't it fun?" Her hazel eyes were shining.

"It's fantastic," Trixie agreed, "but—"

"I know, you want to find out more about the necklace," Honey guessed. She and Trixie often understood each other without talking.

"And tie up a few other odds and ends," Trixie added.

When the Bob-Whites took their seats in the Royal Shakespeare Theatre, Trixie was still thinking of Gray Cap bottled up in Warwick Castle. But when the play began, she forgot all about him. Caught up

183

in the magic spell of *A Midsummer Night's Dream*, she was in another world till the houselights came up for intermission.

"It's almost as good as our Sleepyside Junior-Senior High production," Jim chuckled as they filed out to the lobby to get their ices.

"Don't let Gregory hear you say that," said Honey.

After the play, Gregory joined them for a late supper at the Dirty Duck, where actors gathered after shows, and tourists gathered to see the actors. Gregory's cheeks were rosy with makeup he had only hastily removed.

"Jeepers, imagine having supper with Thisbe," Trixie giggled.

"You were great," Honey told him shyly.

"Good show, old chap," Mart couldn't resist saying, in a pompous voice.

Ordinarily Gregory's voice, like his father's, was very deep, but as Thisbe he had used a high, squeaky voice. He entertained the Bob-Whites with some of the lines from his role and then went on to mimic other roles. " 'I have had a dream,' " he told them in Bottom's braying voice, " 'past the wit of man to say what dream it was.' "

"Wasn't it a wonderful evening?" Trixie said to Honey, after they got back to the Rose Room and were getting ready for bed. "I'll never forget this trip to England as long as I live."

"Even if we don't solve our case?" Honey teased.

"Well," admitted Trixie, "I'll be more apt to remember it if we do get this case wrapped up."

Trixie woke up so early that the birds hadn't even started to sing. It was barely light.

This is our last day, she thought. She didn't want to waste a minute of it.

"Honey?" She reached over to the other bed and poked the heap under the covers. "Are you awake?"

Honey rolled over. "Ummm-mm," she said drowsily. "Wha—time—is—it?"

"Time to wake up," Trixie said firmly. "I've got everything figured out. You know how you go to sleep with a problem, and your subconscious works on it? Well, I must have had just the right dreams last night, because—"

"Trixie Belden!" Honey sat up on her elbow and forced her eyes open wide enough to see the clock. "It's not even five o'clock! What in the world are we going to do till breakfast?"

"Talk about the case." Trixie was propped up on her pillows, her blue eyes sparkling. "We won't have any time later. We have to pack, and your mother's coming—what time is she coming?"

"She didn't say," Honey said sleepily.

"We *have* to get to the castle by one," Trixie said.

Honey resigned herself to the idea of staying awake and swung her feet to the floor. "I should think we ought to stay away from that horrible man," she pointed out, "not chase after him. So he tried to get

185

my necklace. He didn't get it, did he? And there wasn't all that much in my handbag, Trix. He can have it. I never want to see that horrid little man again."

"Why does everybody think we ought to let him go," Trixie complained, "when he's important to our case? Maybe he knows something about the necklace that we don't."

"How could he possibly know anything about it? He hasn't even seen it."

"I don't know how," Trixie admitted. "But why would he follow us all the way from London if he didn't know *something*?"

"He probably thinks it's more valuable than it is," Honey said. "He must think the jewels are real, and we did say my necklace looked like Queen Elizabeth's in the Wax Museum."

"Not as much as it looks like the one in Warwick Castle!" Trixie said enthusiastically. "I think we ought to take your necklace along with us and compare it with the one in the portrait. If your mother gets here in time, maybe she could go along—then she could see it's the same, too. And she might persuade the guard to let us get up closer."

"Sure," Honey said, "then out pops Gray Cap from behind a knight in armor, and this time he gets the necklace."

"No, sir, this time *we* get *him*," Trixie said. "We catch him with the goods, so nobody can say we can't prove anything. We'll have Jim and Mart with us, and Gregory wants to go along. There's scads of us, but only one of him. I think."

"You think—what's that supposed to mean?" When Trixie wanted to, she could sound very mysterious, and Honey leaned forward, totally wide-awake.

A Strange Disappearance • 16

THAT'S WHAT I'VE been trying to tell you," said Trixie. "I must have been dreaming about the case last night, and that's what my subconscious came up with—that the pieces of the puzzle don't quite fit together unless—unless there's more than one person in on it."

"Oh, woe," Honey groaned, rolling back onto the bed. "After we leave, they're going to change the name of this room from the Rose Room to the Nut Room! Are you trying to tell me that there's more than one pickpocket after us?" Then she turned serious. "Come to think of it, Trix, you've seen Gray Cap more times than any of the rest of us have. *Is* he more than one person?"

"I'm still kind of hazy about it in my own mind," admitted Trixie. "I'm going to have to think about it some more. Tell you what—let's get up and pack now so we can get that over with. Then we could go over to the stables and see if Gregory's there and if he'll let us go riding before breakfast."

When the girls arrived at the stables an hour later, they found Jim and Gregory saddling up for a ride.

"Where's Mart?" asked Trixie.

"Buried under a pillow," Jim chuckled.

Gregory insisted that the girls and Jim take out the three horses. "My father's too busy to ride this morning," he said, "and I really should get on with my chores. There's something I want to be sure to attend to before you leave for the States."

Now, that *sounds mysterious*, Trixie thought as Gregory strode off.

The country air was exhilarating, and the three riders were a few minutes late for breakfast. Trixie was about to announce that she was as hungry as a horse, when Andrew Hart appeared in the entrance to the Crimson Room. *I bet he can hardly wait for us to go back to America*, Trixie thought.

"Let me know when you are ready to check out," he told them, then turned on his heels and left as abruptly as he had come.

"I hope he didn't mind my riding Black Prince." Jim looked worried. "Gregory said his father almost always rides the stallion himself, but he had too much to do today to get ready for the 'hordes of barbarians' he expects tomorrow.''

"Poor Mr. Hart," Honey said. "I think it's terrible that he has to take in tourists when he hates it so much."

"Anne says he'll get used to it," Mart said. "She told me it takes him a long time to adjust to change. When his wife died, he almost had a breakdown. So I don't think his attitude toward us is anything personal. Another thing Anne told me while you were out prancing around was that she told Gregory last night about Honey's necklace matching the one in the castle. He says he has an idea about Honey's necklace, but he wants to check it out before telling us. That's where he's gone now."

"What kind of an idea?" Trixie was bursting with questions. "How's he going to check it out? Can he do it before Mrs. Wheeler gets here?"

"I believe there's someone he wants to talk to at the theater," Mart said, "but I'm not sure."

"At the theater," Honey said thoughtfully. "I wonder what he could find out there."

Trixie was so excited she could hardly finish her breakfast. "When's he coming back? Do you think he can find out why they copied the necklace? Maybe somebody wanted to steal the real one and—"

"Calm down, old girl," Mart said, "before you drive us all bonkers."

Miss Trask and McDuff had eaten earlier than the

Bob-Whites and were saying their good-byes out in the vestibule. McDuff was planning on taking the late morning bus to Glasgow. After breakfast, the Bob-Whites went out to say good-bye, and soon the tall Scotsman was waving heartily at them from a taxi. He was leaving the Maroon Saloon there, to be picked up by the rental company later.

Trixie heaved a sigh of relief, but there were tears in Honey's eyes. *Honey and I probably never will agree about that man*, thought Trixie as they all went back into the house.

Miss Trask went straight to her room. "I must get a letter off to my sister," she said. "I've been so frightfully busy, but I did want it to have a Stratford postmark."

"She's as bad as my brother," Trixie whispered to Honey. "Ten days in England and he'll never talk the same. And anyway, I figured she'd be taking McDuff to the bus station, to see him off."

"She probably just wants to be by herself for a little while," Honey said.

The housekeeper, Mrs. Hopkins, entered and informed Honey that she had a telephone call.

"It was Mother," Honey said when she came back moments later. "She won't be arriving till late afternoon, and she'd like to spend the night here tonight. She could probably have McDuff's room, I told her. Then we'll meet my father in London tomorrow morning and fly back to New York."

191

"One more night in England," Trixie said happily.

The Bob-Whites decided that there was time for a cruise on the Avon that morning. Gregory was still at the theater, but to everyone's surprise, Anne was free to accompany them.

"Here go my last two shillings," said Trixie as the Bob-Whites and Anne paid their admissions and boarded the *Swan of Avon.*

It was a lovely ride—through a canal, under the old stone bridge, past private estates with beautiful gardens that sloped down to the river. At one of the woven wood fences, a little boy stood all alone, watching wistfully as the merry boatload passed by under huge chestnut trees and weeping willows.

"Poor little rich boy," Honey murmured. "I used to be lonesome like that, before we moved to Sleepyside and I met Trixie, and we found Jim, and started the Bob-Whites—"

"And here we are chugging along on the *Swan of Avon,*" Trixie marveled. "Can you believe it?"

When they got back to Hartfield House, Gregory was there. He had news for them about the necklace, he said, but he seemed worried about something else. "Where's Father?" he asked Anne.

"I haven't the foggiest," she said.

The housekeeper had been expecting Mr. Hart to go over her shopping list with her. "I've searched the house from top to bottom," she said. " 'Tisn't like him to go off like that."

"Could he have decided to go riding, after all?" Jim asked. "Have you checked the stables?"

Jim grinned modestly when Gregory clapped him on the back. "Bully for you, old fellow," Gregory said. "That's exactly where he'll be."

Sure enough, when they reached the stables, Mr. Hart's handsome black stallion was missing. The Bob-Whites decided to stay and help Gregory with some chores he had put off when he'd gone to inquire about Honey's necklace.

"Well, what did you find out?" Trixie burst out at the first possible moment.

"Come now," Mart said, "don't pop your blooming cork!"

"What's the bloke talkin' about?" Gregory dead-panned back. When everybody had finished laughing, he told them that he had consulted with the curator at the Royal Shakespeare Theatre Museum. "It occurred to me that Honey's necklace might have been used as costume jewelry in Shakespeare's plays," he said.

"Gleeps," Trixie cried immediately, "so that's what it was for!"

"It was just an idea," Gregory cautioned. "But the curator at the museum is rather keen on getting a look at the piece. If the fake necklace *is* a duplicate of the queen's, it could have been copied from the portrait in Warwick Castle, if not from the actual necklace."

"What are we waiting for?" Trixie demanded. "Let's go get the necklace."

"Good-o!" Anne's eyes were shining. "I'll open the safe for you, since Father isn't here."

"I'll be with you in a jiff," said Gregory. "I just have to finish grooming the horses."

"Need any more help?" Jim asked hopefully.

Jim decided to stay with Gregory, and Mart followed the girls to the rear hallway of Hartfield House, where the safe stood behind the check-in counter. Anne had no trouble with the combination, but just as the heavy iron door swung open, the housekeeper came hurrying out of the kitchen.

"Did you find Mr. Hart?" she asked anxiously.

"Oh, yes, Mrs. Hopkins," Anne assured her. "He went riding, after all. I'm sure he'll be back shortly."

Ignoring Mrs. Hopkins, the three Bob-Whites were staring incredulously into the open safe.

It was empty!

At the Castle Gate • 17

WHILE ANNE RANG up the constable, Mart tore up the stairs to tell Miss Trask, and Trixie and Honey raced to the stables to get Jim.

"We've got to get Miss Trask to take us to the station before the bus leaves," Trixie told Honey breathlessly.

"The bus? You mean—"

"Of course! It had to be McDuff. There's nobody else it could be," Trixie panted as they sped across the field.

There was no sign of Jim or Gregory at the stables.

"Where could they be?" Honey was bewildered. "If they're not here, we should have met them on their way back. I hope nothing's wrong."

"This is very strange," Trixie said slowly. "Black Prince is in his stall. I thought they said he was gone."

"He was! That's how they figured out where Mr. Hart was," Honey said. "And now the other two horses are gone instead. But Trixie, what did you mean about Mr. Mc—"

"Can't talk now," Trixie interrupted. "Can't wait either."

Even Honey's long legs could hardly keep up as Trixie fairly flew back to the house. Mart was just coming downstairs with Miss Trask, and Anne was still talking to the constable.

"You say the necklace is missing?" Miss Trask was asking in her no-nonsense way. "I'm sure there's some explanation. Where's Mr. Hart?"

"He's missing, too," Trixie announced, catching her breath.

"He went riding," Honey said.

"Only his horse is back, and now we can't find him or Jim—"

"Or Gregory or their horses, either," Honey said anxiously.

"The boys must have gone for a ride, but *we've* got to get to that bus station before McDuff gets away," concluded Trixie.

"Since when have you decided that we couldn't get along without Mr. McDuff?" Miss Trask asked a bit sharply. Trixie couldn't quite look at her.

"Trixie thinks he did it." Honey's voice quavered. "Took the necklace, I mean."

"And whatever else was in the safe," Trixie added. "Come on—let's hurry!"

"Trixie Belden, I don't follow your logic," said Miss Trask sternly. "Whatever else he may be, Gordie McDuff is certainly no thief."

"In any case," Mart said diplomatically, "we sure could use his help right now, couldn't we, Trix?" He threw her a warning look.

"Uh, right," Trixie hastily agreed. "He must know something about what's going on. It can't do any harm to catch up with him and see what he knows."

"You probably have a point there," said Miss Trask. "Although, well—to be totally honest, I was rather counting on never seeing that man again."

Trixie, Honey, and Mart stared at each other in astonishment.

"He was a nice enough man," Miss Trask went on, "and I am fond of a Scottish brogue. But frankly, he and his accent were beginning to wear on my nerves. I had no intention of seeing him once we were back in New York."

It was not Miss Trask's habit to confide in the Bob-Whites, but Trixie wasn't marveling at that. Something else was clicking inside her brain.

"Miss Trask, *please* trust me," she cried. "We haven't got time for any more explanations—we have

197

to get to the station immediately!"

"Very well," agreed Miss Trask.

Anne stayed behind to wait for the constable, but the others headed out to the Maroon Saloon, which was conveniently pointed toward town. Mart got in beside Miss Trask in the front, and Trixie and Honey climbed into the backseat. Miss Trask turned the key in the ignition.

The motor gave no response.

"I don't understand," said Miss Trask. "It's been running like a charm all week." She got out, lifted the hood, and peered around in the engine.

Trixie would have been racing around the grounds, trying to find another car, but she knew as well as anyone that there were very few machines that fazed the versatile manager of the Wheeler estate.

Ten minutes later, the Maroon Saloon was purring again.

"A disconnected wire," Miss Trask said as she steered the car out of the driveway.

Trixie leaned forward. "Do you think it was sabotage?"

"Wires normally don't disconnect themselves," Miss Trask replied shortly.

Honey looked miserable, and even Trixie couldn't bring herself to accuse McDuff aloud. Everyone was silent while Miss Trask drove the car over the old stone bridge and into the parking lot of the bus station. The last morning bus for Glasgow was revving up for departure, and a few late passengers scurried aboard as Trixie and Mart jumped out of the car.

It occurred to Trixie that she had absolutely no idea of what she was going to say to McDuff when they caught him, but she brushed the thought away. *I'll think of something*, she assured herself.

Ignoring the bus driver's demand for tickets, the two Beldens hopped on board and began making their way through the narrow aisle of the bus. Passengers were still stowing their luggage in the compartments overhead, and it seemed to take forever for Trixie and Mart to reach the rear of the bus. They saw no sign of their former guide.

"How could I be so stupid?" Trixie cried. "He's conned us again!"

"He must have never had any intention of taking this bus," agreed Mart.

"Or of going to Scotland," Trixie said. "But now I know where he *is* going! Come on, Mart!

"If we hurry," she told Miss Trask as she and Mart scrambled back into the Maroon Saloon, "we can still get to the castle before the gate opens."

"The *castle?*" Everyone except Trixie was bewildered, and Trixie's mile-a-minute explanation wasn't that helpful. Fortunately, Miss Trask took one look at Trixie's face and set off for Warwick.

"Now, suppose you start from the beginning," Miss Trask said once the car was speeding past old brick farmhouses and flocks of woolly sheep.

199

Trixie took a deep breath. "You see, it had to be McDuff who stole Honey's necklace," she began. "He's the only one besides the Harts and their housekeeper who was there this morning. Mr. Hart is not exactly my favorite person, but I can't imagine Anne's father being a thief. He doesn't even want to take people's money for staying in his house—he's too proud. And it couldn't have been Gray Cap this time, because he was locked up in the castle."

Miss Trask pressed her lips into a thin line and kept her eyes on the road. "Your logic leaves much to be desired," she said. "If Mr. McDuff is the culprit, why are we going to Warwick Castle? Won't he be heading straight for London, where he can disappear?"

Trixie shook her head violently. "He has to go to the castle first."

"But why?" Honey persisted. "You don't think he'd have the nerve to try to steal the queen's portrait, too, do you?"

"No, no, no!" Trixie's curls bounced with every word. "Remember, Honey, I told you this morning that more than one person is involved in this case?"

Honey nodded, and Trixie went on. "McDuff was in Oxford, for example, when the Rose Room was ransacked, but we know Gray Cap was in Stratford that day! And I haven't told this to anyone yet because I knew you would think I was crazy, but I heard voices on the battlements when I followed McDuff up the tower after we saw Gray Cap go in there. McDuff must have been telling the pickpocket to lie low till he could get the necklace when he checked out at Hartfield House this morning. Don't you see? They're in cahoots!"

"But you didn't actually see them talking to each other, did you?" Mart asked. "Did you ever see Gray Cap up there on the parapet?"

"No, but McDuff wouldn't let me look around. He practically forced me down the stairs—"

"But how would Mr. McDuff get the necklace?" Honey interrupted. "That safe wasn't cracked."

"That's what I've been worried about," Trixie admitted. "You know that big fat roll of bills he asked Anne to put in the safe for him when we all checked our valuables? Well—"

"Somebody had to open the safe for him when he checked out!" Mart slapped his knee. "Trixie, you're a whiz!"

"But in order to steal the necklace and clean out the whole safe," Trixie said soberly, "he must have had to pull a gun or something."

"Oh, *Trixie*," Honey protested.

Miss Trask pressed her foot down harder on the accelerator. "You don't think anything has happened to Andrew Hart?"

"That's the part I can't figure out." Trixie frowned. "The housekeeper couldn't find him—that was after McDuff checked out—but then we figured he'd gone riding, since his horse was gone. But now

Black Prince is back, and all three of them have disappeared—Jim, Gregory, *and* Mr. Hart."

"So McDuff has to stop by the castle to pick up the pickpocket, right, Trix?" Mart said. "And if we catch up with him, he'll have to give us some answers."

"Right. He's probably hired another car," Trixie said. "Won't he be surprised when we drive up in the Maroon Saloon—which he thought he had put out of commission!"

"He was certainly lying about being an experienced mechanic," Miss Trask sniffed. "Now, if he had removed the rotor from under the distributor cap, *that* might have stumped me."

"But—if he has a gun—" Honey shivered.

"I do wish Jim and Gregory were here," Trixie said. "But it's still four against two. And we don't really know that he has a gun. He could have found some other way to threaten Mr. Hart."

"We have five minutes before the gate opens," Miss Trask said briskly, parking the Maroon Saloon in a lot around the corner from the castle. In thirty seconds, she and the Bob-Whites had joined the long queue of Sunday afternoon tourists.

"I don't see anything of Mr. McDuff," Miss Trask said. "Trixie, perhaps there's some other explanation for the disappearance of the necklace. Something quite innocent."

Honey brightened visibly. "Maybe Mr. Hart, Jim, and Gregory took it to show to that curator of the

Royal Shakespeare Museum."

"I'm afraid not," Mart muttered under his breath. "Shrink into the crowd, everybody, and look over there!"

McDuff was getting out of a black car he had just parked across the street from the castle. Not seeming to notice the Bob-Whites or the Maroon Saloon, he strode toward the castle, whistling "And I'll be in Scotland afore ye."

Trixie's blue eyes shot sparks. "Oh, ye will, will ye?" she whispered.

McDuff's gaze was fastened on the heavy timber gate as the porter swung it wide. A crowd of tourists poured in, but Trixie put her finger on her lips and motioned the others to hold back. McDuff bought his ticket and walked through the arch.

"We'll stop them on the way out," she said. "Both of them."

"Good thinking," Mart agreed.

Honey was hanging on to Miss Trask's arm, and they both looked unhappy. Trixie was sorry that they were being disillusioned, and she was still worried about Anne's father, but nothing could suppress the feeling of exhilaration that always came over her whenever the Bob-Whites were closing in on a criminal like Gordie McDuff. *If only Jim were here*, she thought. *We really need him.*

It was Miss Trask who suggested a thorough search of McDuff's new car for any evidence that he might have inadvertently left behind.

"Not the jewels, of course," she said. "He wouldn't leave them in the car. But there might be something we could use to persuade the police he should be arrested. Otherwise he's likely to talk them right out of it. You three keep your eye on the exit. I'll be right back."

"What a super idea!" Trixie exclaimed.

"Sure is," said Mart, turning back to the gate. "Are you sure you don't want to call it the Trask-Belden-Wheeler Detective Agency?"

It seemed like hours, but Trixie's watch said one-thirty when McDuff and Gray Cap finally appeared around a bend in the winding, stone-walled drive. The gray, scar-faced man wasn't wearing his cap, but Trixie would have known him anywhere, from that furtive, sidling walk with which he slipped through crowds. At the moment, however, the crowds were all inside the castle. Trixie, Honey, Mart, and Miss Trask were alone except for the young English porter.

"There they come!" Trixie told the porter.

"Trixie, you are not to take any chances," Miss Trask said crisply. She was the first to step forward as McDuff and the pickpocket approached the only public exit from Warwick Castle.

McDuff's black eyes wavered for a fraction of a second as they met her furious blue ones. Then he broke into a grin. "Marge," he said heartily. "Sure, and I thought I had seen the last of ye—that is, ah"—he floundered at the expression on her face—"till we meet again—in America."

Miss Trask's short gray hair fairly bristled as she held out her hand, palm up. "Now, if you'll give me Honey's necklace," she said tersely.

McDuff hung his head like a schoolboy caught throwing erasers. He reached into his pocket, but the sparkle of silver that flashed as his hand came out was no necklace.

"Watch it!" Trixie screamed. "It's a knife!"

Gray Cap produced another, and the two men motioned the Bob-Whites and Miss Trask over to the porter's station.

"I dinna want to hurt anybody," McDuff assured them. "But just to make certain that ye give us a good start, we'll take one of ye along with us. How about the bonny lass, eh, Ferdie?" he asked Gray Cap.

Trixie was trembling, but she stepped forward obediently as the pickpocket singled her out with his switchblade.

All's Well That Ends Well · 18

MISS TRASK SPOKE UP firmly. "You are certainly not taking anyone hostage. If you are thinking of adding to the charges against you, kindly remember that kidnapping is a very serious crime."

McDuff and Ferdie conferred for a moment and then slowly backed away, their knives still pointed at the Bob-Whites, Miss Trask, and the porter. "Don't move, any of you," McDuff snarled without a trace of an accent. "I'm already faced with armed robbery, and I don't need any other charges. But I won't hesitate to use this."

Honey clutched Trixie's hand as the two men backed across the deserted street to the black car and got inside. McDuff slid behind the wheel, and Ferdie sat in the seat next to him, glaring evilly at the little group by the gate.

Trixie gritted her teeth. "We can't just stand here," she cried. "They're getting away with the necklace!" She couldn't decide whether to scream bloody murder or throw herself in front of the car.

"That necklace isn't worth one second of your precious lives," Miss Trask said quietly.

Miss Trask was right, and Trixie knew it. "Gleeps," she groaned, "I must be growing up. I'm getting *sensible*."

"I doubt they'll get far," the young porter said hopefully. "I've alerted the castle guards. There's a small button under the counter, you see."

"And here comes the local constabulary," Mart whooped as the familiar *a—hoo—a—hoo* of the English police horns rang out through Warwick.

"There's Jim!" Trixie shrieked as the tall, red-haired boy came running toward them.

"Am I glad you're all safe!" He threw his arms around Trixie and whirled her until she was dizzy.

For a moment, Trixie's eagle eye was off the robbers. When she looked back, the black car was still at the curb, and McDuff and Ferdie were outside, looking under the hood. Two honking police cars roared around the corner.

"How about that?" Trixie gasped. "They can't even get started!"

Miss Trask looked pleased as the constables penned in the black car and took the thieves into custody. The two men gave up without a fight.

"I do believe that someone has removed the rotor from under the distributor cap," their chaperon chuckled.

"Miss Trask!" the Bob-Whites chorused.

"Jeepers, is she a good sport!" Trixie whispered to Honey.

Honey was looking past Trixie at Gregory and Anne, who had come up behind Jim. "Is your father okay?" she asked anxiously.

"He seems to be," said Anne, smiling.

"McDuff gave him a hard time, though," Jim said. "He pulled the gun as soon as Mr. Hart got the safe open, and then he forced him out to the stables."

"I thought it took McDuff a long time to come down to the vestibule with his luggage," Miss Trask said.

Gregory nodded. "He let Black Prince out to make it look like my father had gone riding. Then he knocked out my father and dragged him behind a pile of hay. When Black Prince came back without a rider, I thought my father had been thrown, and so Jim and I rode out to look for him."

"So that's why nobody was in the stables when we came to look for Jim," Trixie said.

"Only there *was* someone there," said Honey, shuddering.

"Poor Mr. Hart!" Trixie exclaimed. "No wonder he doesn't think much of tourists—look what happened to him when he took us in! I hope there's some way we can make it up to him."

As the whole group headed back to the parking lot, Trixie filled in Jim, Anne, and Gregory on how she had figured out that McDuff and Gray Cap had been working together all along. "It was Gray Cap who first spotted us in the Wax Museum," she decided. "He overheard Honey talking about her necklace and tried to swipe it. Failing that, he started following us."

Like Gregory and Honey, Jim was full of admiration for Trixie's detective skills. "So McDuff was Gray Cap's smooth-talking partner," he mused.

"Right," said Trixie. "You could tell that everything that man said, true or false, was designed to gain our confidence so he could be our guide and tell Gray Cap where we were going to be." She was silent for a moment. "And Miss Trask, what you said before about a Scottish brogue reminded me of something else Gray Cap overheard us saying in the Wax Museum. We were talking about how bloody Scottish and English history was, and Jim said something about you liking the sound of the Scottish accent. So that's why McDuff talked with one—only it was fake, like everything else about him!"

"No wonder it got on my nerves," Miss Trask said.

Honey still looked troubled. "Trixie thinks that

either McDuff or Gray Cap pushed me off that curb in Piccadilly Circus so that McDuff could pretend to save me," she said unhappily. "But I just can't believe that anyone would do such a horrible thing."

"Maybe he was just an opportunist," Mart suggested seriously.

"What do you mean?"

"He could have been making the best of an opportunity that came his way," said Jim. "With both guys keeping tabs on us, they probably figured that sooner or later something was going to happen that would give McDuff the chance to gain our confidence. So maybe McDuff really did save your life, Honey."

Honey rewarded the boys with a radiant smile.

"I guess we'll never know for sure," said Trixie, leaning against the Maroon Saloon. "I just can't get over how much trouble those two took to get at a necklace. They must have assumed it was horrendously valuable. That reminds me," she said, turning to Gregory, "did you find out anything more from the curator at the theater museum?"

"I've invited him to dinner tonight so he can examine the necklace after we get it back from the police and before you take it back to the States," said Gregory. "That is, if you have no objection."

"I'm just thankful we have the necklace to show him," Honey said. "And Mother will be here for dinner, too. She'll be fascinated at what we've been able to find out—that the necklace was copied from Queen Elizabeth's and used in Shakespeare's plays."

"I'm afraid that's only a hypothesis," said Gregory. "But Mr. Cowles, the curator, told me he wished he had the funds to purchase a historical piece like that for the museum. Unfortunately, he's barely able to keep the museum going. We all depend a great deal on the generosity of foreign visitors, though people like my father find that a hard pill to swallow."

"Well, I think it's a perfectly marvelous hypotenuse," Trixie said enthusiastically. "And I'll bet Mrs. Wheeler will be so thrilled that she'll let Honey *give* the necklace to the museum!"

Everyone groaned at Trixie's rendition of "hypothesis"—and even more at her impetuous offer of the Hart family heirloom. Everyone, that is, but Honey.

"That's a super idea," she said, smiling at Gregory and Anne.

"Father will be terribly impressed if you do something like that," Anne told her. "That's bound to convince him that tourists are absolutely smashing."

"*Some* tourists, at any rate," said Gregory warmly.

"You and Anne will have to come to Sleepyside-on-the-Hudson sometime," Honey said, "to visit your American cousins."

"That's all of us Bob-Whites," Trixie told them, "including some you haven't even met yet."

"International relations seem to be looking up, old girl," said Mart with an infuriating grin at Trixie.

211

"About time, eh, what? Jolly good, I'd say."

"Eh, Mart," Jim spoke up suddenly, "I just recalled a quote from the Bard that seems particularly applicable to you. It's 'brevity is the soul of wit.' Get it?" he asked teasingly.

"Got it," said Mart. "But that reminds me of another famous quote. It goes something like 'mystery is the soul of Trix.' Got that?"

Trixie wasn't about to let her brother have the last word on the subject, and besides, she'd remembered a Shakespeare quote of her own. "Well," she replied tartly, "as I've always said, 'to thine own self be true!' " Before Mart could respond, she opened the door of the Maroon Saloon and hopped inside.